Gabriela

Tales From A Demon Cat

By

R.C. Rumple

This book is a work of fiction. References to real people, events, establishments, organizations, or locales are intended only to provide a sense of authenticity and are used fictitiously. All other characters, and all incidents and dialogue, are drawn from the author's imagination and are not construed as real.

ISBN-13: 978-1722320966

ISBN-10: 1722320966

PUBLISHER'S NOTES

My Thanks

Usually, I start off this page of gratitude by naming the many advance readers who assist me in discovering areas of weakness and strength. Yet, this time, the list is much too long. With the many various stories enclosed, my readers were given the opportunity to read only a few, and none have read all. I do wish to say a hearty "Thank You" to each who participated in the reading of my works and for the assistance they rendered.

I do wish to express my sincere gratitude to a gentleman, and a fellow herper, who mentored me earlier this year and has become instrumental in taking my writing to the next level. Even though I suspect this publication will not be perfect in his eyes, I am eternally grateful to Jason V. Brock for opening my eyes in many ways to give the reader a more pleasurable reading experience. He deserves my full respect for taking on the challenge and continues to help me every way he can. I thank you for mentoring me, as well as being my friend, Jason. Maybe one day, I'll make you proud.

Lastly—and once again—I must thank my dear wife. Millie, you put up with my jokes, my sarcasm, and constant, "Hush, I'm writing" comments. I'm a lucky man to have found you thirty-eight years ago. By the way, dear, Gabriela's litter box needs emptying when you get the chance.

Gabriela

Why Didn't I Get A Dog?

Gabriela entered my life as a favor to a friend. I should have known better.

Brushing aside all small talk upon my arrival, he rushed me to meet his devilish offering. A back bedroom had become Gabriela's den, acrid in smell and kept dark with lights off and curtains closed tight. I sought to locate my soon to be "pet" but was unsuccessful until two glowing eyes peered out from under the bed. Pulling me back, my friend whispered, "Give her room. You'll be happy you did."

Black as the bowels of Hell from where she came, Gabriela's appearance as a spawn of Satan confirmed her origin as she stalked about her den, glaring up occasionally as if I were her next meal. I stepped forward to pet her in hopes that she would respond favorably but was met with a maniacal howl and hisses of violent intentions.

I was informed that Gabriela's personality would improve when she no longer had others of her own kind around. She was a loner, one that had no need of company. He spoke of how his other felines had discovered her personality was not to be challenged. Doing so had only led to speedy but fierce battles and medical attention to tend wounds caused by her razor-sharp claws.

"But, I swear to you, she'll get better once she's away from the others. Gabriela will make you a great companion. Unlike a dog, you don't have to keep her amused with fetching a ball. There's no need for long walks twice a day, just a litter box and she's taken care of. And, you won't have neighbors complaining about the barking. Cats don't bark!"

There are many things in life we do that we later regret. The adage, "hindsight is 20/20" comes back to haunt at times. I think back now at how desperate he seemed to make Gabriela mine. His enthusiasm when I said, "Yes" was beyond that of a man finding an unwanted pet a new home. Instead, it was more like the relief of a teenage boy being told no baby was on the way—by three different girls.

I have been accused of being naïve at times. There is no doubt now that becoming Gabriela's new owner proved that accusation. I quickly learned that she would not be owned by anyone. She would own them.

The afternoon was sunny. "A good time to take her home," my friend said. "She is at her weakest during the daylight hours, especially when there are no clouds to block the sun." He pulled out a chrome metal cat carrier and begged her to enter. Wary of his requests, the feline turned away, taking protective cover once again under the bed. I stood back, shaking my head, as he struggled to force her into the cage.

What the hell am I getting myself in for?

Finally latching the door, he sat back on the floor, panting heavy as the sweat poured down his forehead. His slacks--stained red from the blood oozing from the scratches on his hands and forearm--were themselves shredded from the hind paws seeking to maim. As he lit a cigarette and blew smoke at Gabriela in revenge, she exhaled a yellowish smoke, smelling of sulfur, and sent it his direction. I began to regret my decision.

During the journey home, her demonic moans and hisses filled the inside of my car. Music had no chance as her volume surpassed that of my stereo. Besides, I already had the soundtrack to a movie on exorcisms being supplied by my new pet. Noticing some of the cage bars bending from her efforts to escape, I stepped on the gas.

She's just scared. When we get home, she'll calm down. Once she has a good meal, the anger and fear will leave, and she'll be just like any other cat.

I told you I was prone to being naïve.

Parking in my driveway, I reached for the carrier handle but found claws straining through the bars to reach my fingers. I grabbed a set of pliers from the trunk, latched them tight, and carried her inside. Setting it down in the center of the living room, Gabriela hunched against the back of the cage. Figuring her far enough away, I unlatched the door, barely pulling my hand away in time to escape her springing through with claws intending to rip my fingers apart.

Free, Gabriela faced me, black fur standing on end, back arched high, with hisses hurled in my direction. She was determined to make a first impression. But, so was I.

Gathering my bravery, I spoke to her in a calm manner. “Aww, is Gabriela scared? There's no reason to be frightened, you're home. I'm going to take good care of you and show you all the love you deserve. You won't have to fight with other cats to eat. There’s no sharing of the food bowl. You can eat in peace.”

Her hisses increased in quantity and intensity. Crouching as a tiger ready to leap upon prey, there was no hiding her intentions if I made the wrong move. I kept talking, not in standard “talk to the kitty” manner, but intelligently, as I would to a human. Silently I prayed that she would accept my hospitality and bribes.

Minutes dragged, each seeming to take forever to pass. Gabriela’s attack mode eased, and her eyes changed from a red to a yellow glow. Padding off to my favorite chair, she reared high upon her hind legs, stretching high to embed her front razor-sharp claws into my favorite chair. I could only cringe as the leather was sliced from top to bottom. She repeated her act on all four corners until the foam cushion and cloth padding hung from the jagged tears. Finished, she sat facing me, a sadistic smile forming upon her face, waiting for me to react.

For several minutes, neither of us stirred. I wanted to lash out and chastise her, yet, if I did any progress made would be lost. This cat was smarter than any I’d ever dealt with. She was attempting to psyche me out, get me angry, see how I'd retaliate. If I showed my ire, she'd know I would be a combatant as long as she stayed. If I showed her vandalism had no effect on me, maybe she'd recognize my efforts to appease any further confrontations. Maybe I was giving her too much credit and being naïve, again.

Finally, she rose to her feet and took refuge in the makeshift cave between the couch and the wall—her choice of homeland—later named "The Den of Evil."

I took refuge in the kitchen and found temporary solace in a bottle of lite beer. *This cat is a wild beast, a crazed lunatic, a demon! I've got to get her on my side somehow. Let me put out some food and see what happens. Maybe she'll eat the kitty chow instead of me.*

I slept with my bedroom door locked that night. The bitter smell of sulfur seeped through the gap underneath the door reminding me that these were her hours of "strength" and she'd be weaker in the morning. I was awakened several times by the same moans heard during the drive home, only much louder. It was as if a door to Hell had opened and the agony of the tortured held me captive to its sadistic pleasures. Pulling the covers over my head, I revisited the "safety of the blankets" concept my parents had taught me during my younger days, knowing it untrue, but having no other option to explore.

"She's at her weakest during the daylight hours." My ex-friend's words echoed in my head as I lay waiting the last few minutes before morning arrived. Usually, I shun the sunlight, wanting to remain in bed and enjoy its softness and warmth. Yet, when the sun's rays finally shone through the window, I greeted them with a smile.

The smell of sulfur was gone, along with the moans that had plagued the night. Hoping for the best, I left the safety of my locked room, took a shower, and dressed before heading out to face the beast.

"I'll be damned, what did you do in here?"

My loveseat was shredded—pieces of foam and cotton strewed throughout the living room. Coffee and end tables lie overturned and scarred with deep gashes and claw marks. Lamps, without shades, all smashed from the bases to the bulbs. And, she'd shown no mercy to the carpet which had been ripped apart in sections leaving only the padding in spots. Even my collection of DVDs had been removed from their cases and destroyed.

From her den, Gabriela slowly appeared and gave me a "Good Morning" hiss, awaiting my response. Somewhat in a state of shock, I did the only thing I could.

Walking to the kitchen, I pulled out a clean bowl and filled it with dry cat food. After washing and filling her water dish, I put both by the doorway to the living room. "If you want something to eat, it's waiting."

The evil queen strolled out of her den, sniffed the dry food, and gave me a glance that said, "I would prefer canned. Maybe, one day, you'll get that through your head. I can be a real bitch if I don't get my way."

"You'll get canned food at night and have a bowl of dry available to you every morning to munch on if you get hungry. No one will touch it, so there's no reason to think you'll ever go hungry." Strangely, her head bobbed, as if she understood and could live with that answer. It was the first major milestone. We had communicated.

I left her alone most of the time in the following days. Being a writer, I spend most of my time typing away, creating stories for my readers. One afternoon, I turned and caught her watching me from across the room. "I'm sure you've heard the old *'curiosity killed the cat'* cliché. Well, you don't have to worry about that here. If you're interested in what I'm doing, or if you simply want a little attention, come over any time and I'll do my best to comply with your wishes. Believe it or not, we can be friends."

Expecting the habitual hiss as a reply, I was surprised as she advanced in my direction and took a seat on what was left of the loveseat arm to my right.

"I don't like people who claim to be my friend. They're just lying. Sooner or later, they toss you out and don't care if you starve or die. People suck."

Okay, this isn't happening. I'm hearing her in my mind. Cats don't talk, and they sure don't have telepathic powers. Damn, I have been alone in the house too long. I'm going crazy!

"I can't attest to that, but cats do talk, or use telepathy as you say. People just don't listen. Why do you think we have the reputation of being so damned independent? If everything you said was ignored, you'd say, "Fuck 'em" and do your own thing, too."

I can't tell you how weird I felt as stunned and amazed don't even come close. This cat, this demon, this creature from Hell was answering my thoughts. Wondering if she understood verbal communication, I asked, "So, should I just think, and you pick up my thoughts, or would it be better for me to talk out loud?"

"Oh, please talk normally," she responded, sounding slightly disgusted at my question. "Your brain is filled with so many worthless thoughts I'd go crazy trying to sort them out. Talk to me and I'll answer you when and if I decide to do so."

With that, Gabriela left my side and returned to her spot behind the couch. That night, the smell of sulfur was gone, as well as the moans that had become commonplace over her short stay. I came close to leaving the door unlocked, but my trust in her was still a little on the light side. Why take chances?

Days passed, and she didn't talk again. In fact, I'd started wondering if she'd ever spoken to me at all. Her life consisted of staying behind the couch most of the daylight hours and lying on the window sill, staring at the moon, during the evening. I fed her as promised, twice a day, and watched as Gabriela's fur began to shine and her frame filled out. She wasn't friendly, but she'd proven to be adept at keeping out of my way. Plus, she had ceased her efforts to destroy every piece of furniture I owned and no longer hissed at me (except when I reached out to pet her).

Late one evening, when my editing of a novel was almost complete, she once again took her place on the loveseat arm. I saw her, extended a quick "Hello" in welcome, and went back to my editing.

"You know, your writing isn't half bad. But, your stories leave much to be desired. The tales I could tell you would make your readers sit back and say, "What in the world did I just read? It was so different!"

"So, you're a writer, too? Have a lot published, do you?"

"Oh, Mr. Smartass here," her sarcasm showing. "I don't waste my time writing. I have better things to do. I simply know a lot of stories, some of my own lives that would make your readers sit up and take notice and some I heard while waiting in line in Hell to be reborn. If you want, I'll tell you a few and you can decide whether to type them out or not. It's up to you."

"What do you mean your own lives?"

"People say that cats have nine lives. They've got it half right. We do have nine lives, but not all during one life. We're born and then reincarnated eight more times before we can rest forever. I'm on my last one. When it's over, that's it. I can leave your kind behind and go to our version of Heaven called Cathala. You know, like the Vikings Valhalla, but there's no one named "Val" there. We'll have plenty of mice to chase, toys to enjoy, and spend our days hanging around enjoying the lazy life."

She was talking again. It was time to ask some questions that had been bothering me. "When you first got here, there was the smell of sulfur and a lot of moans during the night. What was that about?"

"I was pissed off. I'd just gotten the cats at the other place to understand I wasn't someone they wanted to mess with and I'm yanked up, put in a cage, and dropped off here. Not complaining, but you aren't much of a decorator. This place sucks. The sulfur and moans? Simple, when cats die, it depends on what they were doing when they died as to where they spend time waiting in line to be born again. I haven't always been the darling, so I've learned a few things from my visits to Hell. Figured if you didn't work out, they'd provide a reason to find me a home that would."

"Yeah, I loved you at first sight, too," I threw back at her. "Look, these stories you're talking about … you know I'm a writer in the genres of

Horror and Thrillers, right? Will your stories fit my readers?"

She turned her face away and stared out the window at the moon. "Listen, my life has been filled with horror. Plus, a few friends always get together and tell stories while you're waiting to get reborn. Some of my stories will scare you, some will be strange, and others will just freak you out. Do you want to hear one or not?"

Who could say "No" to that?

Kind of Handy

The first human I ever saw was an ugly bastard. I had nothing to compare him to, so I thought all humans looked like him. If a heavy black unibrow, overbearing forehead, and a huge hooked nose were common traits of human appearance, I was happy to be feline.

He caught me in a traumatized state. It was 1947 and mother had been killed by a pair of savage watchdogs only moments before. She had positioned herself between us kittens and the snarling duo hoping to provide her offspring an opportunity to escape. Mother was marvelous, bristling her hair, arching her back, and spitting out hisses that fully announced her intentions to rip the canines to shreds should they come any closer. Unfortunately, so focused was she on the two, an unseen third pounced on her from behind. We scattered, hearing Mother's final cry of pain behind us as powerful jaws crushed her spine.

My brothers skirted off to the right toward a pile of old tires. I ran as fast as my tiny legs would carry me toward the street, hoping they'd lose me in its cavalcade of scents. Perhaps, the blackness of my fur blended with the darkness and kept them from following. Then again, maybe the dogs simply wanted the three-course meal my siblings offered instead of the snack I would supply. Whatever the reason, I'm still haunted to this day by their screams for help and the crunching of bones that came next.

Upon reaching the street, I saw you tall, two-legged creatures up close for the first time. I'd caught prior glimpses of humans from our home in the wooden crate, but that was from a distance. Being new to this world, I wasn't experienced in knowing how distance would affect one's perspective of size. You suckers are giants.

Directly in front of me stood the tall, ugly one I've already described. He seemed to be looking down at me as the dogs had to my mother only seconds before. In defense, I arched my back, copying the position my mother had presented in hopes of scaring him away. In hindsight, I probably should have darted off.

Huge hands lowered and headed my way. I slashed out, but in my haste, missed my target. Strong fingers picked me up by the scruff of my neck and raised me high, directly in front of the beast's face. My hisses only seemed to amuse.

"Ah, such a little creature, all alone in this world—like I am. Put those claws away and let us be friends. We all need companionship, do we not? My name is Victor," he said, turning me so he could check out my gender. *Very embarrassing, I must add.* And you … let's call you Gabriela. Perhaps, Princess Gabriela, if you please. I'm pleased to meet you madame."

In time, I would learn to understand his words. Yet, this was my first life—my first contact with humans—and I only knew the calm, gentle tone of his voice was comforting. The longer he spoke, the more I relaxed. Cradling me against his stomach, we started off down the street, forever leaving the place of my birth and the mangled bodies of my family.

Over the months, we became friends. With no one else to share his love, I was spoiled with all sorts of toys and food treats. I hated to see Victor leave each morning and would be anxious for his day at work to end. He always returned late, but I would be waiting to greet him at the door. I was a glutton for his attention, petting, and listening to his soothing voice. Inseparable, we would eat, me atop the table with my bowl at one end and Victor with his food at the other. Afterward, I'd take my place upon his lap as ballroom music played from the radio. Oh, such fond memories. I still remember his laughter at my attempts to climb onto his bed and how his long fingers would gently lift me and place me atop. We'd sleep until morning, allowing our dreams to entertain us.

Once or twice a month, Victor would spend time in the basement. I didn't know what he was doing there, as he never took me with him. I could hear his voice droning on at times, but nothing was clear enough to make out. No matter, his time there was short, which made me happy.

Gradually, I began to understand the words Victor spoke. They brought about a sadness I hadn't felt since the death of my own family. He would talk to me as if I were human, relating stories of his lonely life. He was a good person, yet, often ignored by those of his kind because of his looks. Destined to be alone, he longed for a normal life—one with a wife and children.

Sitting at the window one evening--watching the birds outside and wanting desperately to chase them—I noticed him strolling up the walk with a female human. She seemed to be injured as Victor was supporting her arm and holding her close. Still, she seemed fine as they entered the house.

"And, this is my fair Gabriela," Victor told his acquaintance, picking me up and giving me a quick hug. "Princess Gabriela has been my friend and companion for several years. You'll be amazed at how intelligent and friendly she is."

"Oh, a cat. I hate cats. They suffocate babies and carry dreadful diseases."

As first impressions go, I had a viable reason to hate this person. Luckily, Victor wasn't swayed by her comments. "Those are only old wives' tales. Gabriela is a darling. I'm sure you'll agree once you get to know her. Gabriela, this is Miss Amy Etheridge, my new friend. I want you to be friends with her."

Yeah, like I was going to reach out and extend my paw to this bitch. To make a point, I showed my fangs and gave her my most vicious hiss. We weren't going to be friends. I'd see to that.

I slept in the living room for the first time that evening. The bedroom door had been closed behind them and no matter how much I pleaded, it stayed shut. I took the hint—life was going to change in Victor's household—and not favorably for me.

The next few months found Amy visiting Victor more often, which meant less time with me. Bored, I would still greet him when he came in the door but found myself getting less attention with Amy swooning in and sweeping him away. Yes, we still listened to the radio, but with her sitting on one side of him and me on the other. He would laugh and joke about being the center of attention and how lucky he was to be loved by two females. I didn't consider it a laughing matter.

Our competition for his attention soon ended. One afternoon, he carried her across the doorway and totally ignored me. *If I could have gotten my claws on her white dress and lace veil, I would have ripped them to shreds.* From that point on, my instrument was second fiddle which I didn't enjoy playing.

Victor was finally happy, though, so I did my best to keep out of Amy's way. I'd find a mouse to toy with and take it to her as a peace offering after killing it. Didn't seem to please her, but I didn't care. I had made the effort. If she didn't want to be friends, that was fine with me.

As Fall arrived, so did a young man knocking at the door. Much younger than Victor, the gentleman was dressed in business attire and carried a brown leather case at his side. Amy smiled as she welcomed him in and offered the young man a seat next to her on the couch. After a few minutes of small talk, he opened his case and began discussing Victor's chances of dying. Next, came his sales pitch about how his insurance company could come to her aid if such a tragedy were to occur.

It was then I noticed how focused her attention was on what the man was saying, as well as giving him multiple "once overs" examining his physical attributes. He was taller than Victor and more slender in stature. His face maintained a look of seriousness, yet, when he managed to smile it was infectious. His vocal tones came close to mimicking Victor's, but were much more captivating, almost hypnotic at times.

Obviously attracted to more than the insurance he offered, Amy inched close to him on the couch. Leaning her shoulder and leg against his, she viewed his presentation materials with interest, and made more than a few hints that she'd like to see his personal items presented.

I had to give the man credit. He continued with his pitch and ignored her suggestions. "Ma'am, I do my best to keep business and pleasure separate. That way, I can give each my best when the occasion arises. Getting back to the plan, if Victor were to die or get killed, you would get all this money."

"I'd be a rich woman if that were to happen," she whispered, lightly nodding. "You sure it would all come to me?"

"Yes, ma'am, it would all come to you. In fact, my company would issue you a check once you presented them with a valid death certificate."

"So, if someone were to break into the house and kill him, it would pay, wouldn't it?"

"Yes, it would. That is, if you had nothing to do with it. Why? You aren't planning on killing your husband, are you?"

His smile at the joke he'd made was met with a serious expression on Amy's face. Catching herself, she forced a smile and a slight giggle. "Who me? Of course not. I wouldn't think of such a thing. Why we've only been married a short time. Seems like forever, but it's only been a few months. Shame … the mistakes we make, isn't it?"

Shocked, I sat in my window seat watching and listening. Mistake? The bitch had taken my place as number one house queen with Victor and she's talking about a mistake? I wanted to leap across the room and slash her sweet little face off. I almost did, but before I could gather myself, the two of them leaned over and started kissing!

I'd love to go on describing all they did, but I'm not one to spread tales, even though I saw a couple of tails spread. I really can't find anything about the human body that would make two people do what they did, but then again, I'm only a feline.

I watched, unable to turn my head away, but I was thinking of Victor. He believed his loneliness was over—a new life in front of him. If he could have seen the two in front of me, he would have been devastated. Amy was only using Victor to improve her place in life. In reality, she was a tramp, a bitch in heat, a slut from the gutter. Victor deserved better.

When he got home that evening, Amy was full of information about the need to get some insurance. Step by step, as if she'd memorized the presentation, she discussed his obligations to her should he be prematurely killed. By dinner's end, he'd agreed to talk to the agent and told her to set up an appointment.

It wasn't hard to see what she was doing. It was a set-up. Somehow, Victor was going to die, and she was going to be rich. Then, she could screw whomever she pleased, be it the insurance guy or someone else. The whole thing was so clear that I was positive of it happening. I needed to tell Victor, but I couldn't talk. I was able to understand their words, but I couldn't speak them, not getting my telepathic abilities until my fifth life. I found frustration almost as hard to deal with as curiosity.

Anyway, the applications were signed, and the policies issued without question. Month after month, the agent, Mr. James Dixon, stopped by the house once a month to collect the premiums and whatever else Amy offered. As expected, James fell in love with her. On a warm spring afternoon, I happened to overhear a conversation as they were putting their clothes back on.

"I wish we could be like this forever—just you and me together," Amy whispered as she pulled up her skirt. "God, you have no idea how much I hate him touching me. Such an ugly man. If I hadn't been without a place to live I never would have agreed to be with him. It's you I want, but as long as he's around it will never happen."

"You could get a divorce. Claim he beats you and you can't take it anymore."

"Do you honestly think a judge would grant me a divorce over that. Maybe one day in they will, but in 1947 it isn't going to happen. A husband can kill his wife and get away with it. No, there's only one way to get away from him."

"Surely, you're not suggesting we do something illegal? Do you think I want to end up in jail the rest of my life?"

"I know you can think of a way to make it happen. That is, if you ever want me again. When you come back next month, I'll expect an answer. Perhaps I will need to find a new insurance man."

I had many reasons to dislike the bitch, but this was one that I couldn't ignore. Somehow, I had to make Victor see Amy's true colors—that she wasn't the sweet thing he thought her to be.

That evening, I jumped up on the table during dinner, where I had eaten with Victor before she had come into the picture. I purposely let my tail drift close to her plate, hoping a stray hair might fly in her food. Several times she told me to get down, and each time I refused Amy's temper came closer to the surface. Finally, she lost it.

"Get down, you little twit. Get your ass off my table!"

Again, I ignored her.

Throwing back her chair, she grabbed a knife and rushed around the table toward me. It took little effort to stay out of her reach until Victor got hold of her from behind.

"Let me go! I'll kill her, I swear I will!"

I sat—my tail end planted on her favorite tablecloth—enjoying her display of raw emotion. She wrestled against Victor's grasp, even threatening him with violence. He held her firmly and kept repeating, "Calm down, my love, calm down" in his most soothing voice. Her attention was elsewhere.

"Damn it, you fucking cat, get your ass down. I swear, as soon as I get free I'm going to skin you alive!"

"Stop this outburst," his voice ordered. "She's only sitting where I used to feed her. Don't blame her, blame me, it's my fault. What's got into you, anyway?"

"I've had about all of the two of you I can stand," Amy blurted out. "I hate her, I hate you, and I hate being here. I wish both of you were dead!" Within a microsecond, she realized what she'd said. Amy went into her act of starting to faint but burst into tears instead. Dropping the knife, she turned and latched hold of Victor, burying her face in his chest. The girl deserved an Academy Award for her performance.

Victor held her close, yet the expression on his face couldn't hide the hurt her words had brought to him. As her tears subsided, he suggested she retire early as she seemed stressed as of late. Passing me on the way to the bedroom, an evil glare came my direction that said, "Wait until we're alone. You're going to pay!"

Alas, being a woman, she was later able to smooth things over with Victor without much trouble. Given the typical excuses—headache, lonely, time of the month, etc.—and Victor was more than willing to forgive. She had brought him happiness and he wasn't willing to lose it.

For over the next few weeks, the only time I spent in the window seat was when Victor was home. Even then, he started spending more time in the basement. The weather had turned chilly, and instead of spending much time outside chopping up wood for the fire, he carried some of the smaller pieces to the basement and split them while he chanted. I felt safe with him in the house, knowing Amy wouldn't try something with him at home. Yet, when Victor was away, I stayed under the couch. It was a tight squeeze, but Amy wasn't strong enough to move the oak framed sofa by herself, so I was safe.

Chance would have it, I was under that sofa sleeping when James showed up the next month. Although dozing, I could make out bits and pieces of a plan he'd devised. It didn't sound good for Victor. In fact, I almost reached out and clawed James' bare knees as he knelt in front of the couch with Amy's legs spread around him after their discussion but decided waiting until a better time would be the right choice.

After James left, Amy hummed a dance tune and whirled around the room with an imaginary partner. "Oh, James, you're such a fool. Who's going to believe your story when I tell them how you'd been after me ever since the first time you stopped by. Just couldn't live without me, could you? Had to kill my husband, who I truly loved, didn't you? I'm going to cry my heart out and get every bit of sympathy the jury can muster before they sentence you. All that money will be mine!"

I stuck my head out and watched her envision the jewels she'd have and the furs she'd be wearing. Traipsing around the room, she fantasized about famous members of society bowing to her beauty and new-found wealth. The bitch was psycho!

I was careless. She caught me staring. "And, Gabriela, you're going to die, too. I'm going to go on a trip after locking you in the house. You'll slowly and painfully starve to death. When I return home, you'll be out of my life, you bitch, out of my life forever!"

James showed up unannounced one December evening. Amy greeted him at the door with a quick kiss and went to the top of the basement steps to let Victor know they had company. Victor soon exited the basement carrying a bundle of kindling. Setting it down by the fireplace, he found he'd absentmindedly brought along the small hatchet he'd been using.

"Victor, I hope you're not planning on using that," James joked.

"No, no, I don't. Must have just have been in a hurry and forgot to put it down. I was splitting a few pieces of wood to get the fire going. It's going to get very cold tonight. Freezing, I'd guess."

James had already spread his materials out upon the dining room table, so Victor took a chair next to him. On completion of the presentation, Amy went to the kitchen to fix some tea for the group.

"So, what do you think? Ready to make this a part of your insurance plan?"

"Actually, I'm thinking of switching to a different company," Victor responded without a blink. "One where I don't have my neighbors telling me how much time the insurance agent spends in my house with my wife every time he visits."

"Sir, what are you insinuating?"

"I'm insinuating nothing," Victor replied, pulling a small pistol from his pocket. "I'm saying that you spend way too much time here to simply be collecting a monthly premium. Do you think me a fool? Now, I'm telling you to get out of my house and never return. If you do, you will never leave."

The blade of the hatchet in Amy's hand fell from behind Victor, slicing through skin and bone and severing the hand from the wrist as it sunk deep within the wooden table top. In the final twitch of a nerve dying, the index finger tightened, pulling the trigger of the revolver. James clutched at his chest and fell back against the wall, blood flowing through his fingers. Dead, he slumped to the floor.

Victor turned to his attacker, "Amy, why? I gave you all I had," his voice was getting weaker.

"Love? What do you know about love, you ugly bastard? Do you know how much I hated looking at you on top of me in bed? I only married you because you caught me at a bad time without any other options. Well, now I have those options thanks to you. I have options and I'll have money. And, I won't have to see you ever again!"

"Oh, yes you will," Victor promised. "Somehow, I'll be back. Somehow, I'll have my revenge. There's a lot you never knew about me—things I didn't want you to know—bad things. I'll be back, just wait." Reaching out with his good hand, he clamped it around her throat.

I sat in my window seat, watching, and hoping he would kill the bitch. I could do nothing to help him accomplish that, or to save him. He was losing too much blood, evident by the large puddle forming on the hardwood floor. A puddle that Amy slipped in and fell into—soaking her from head to toe—and causing Victor to lose his grip.

Amy scrambled away, gasping for breath and Victor fell, weak from the loss of blood. On the floor, he looked up—his eyes reaching into mine—and whispered, "Gabriela, my love, be careful. I'm dying, but she lives. Maybe we'll be together again, soon."

Later that evening, as the morgue people were taking away the bodies and the police were investigating, I squeezed under the sofa to avoid notice—especially Amy's. The police believed it to be a battle between a jealous husband and his wife's lover. Spurting blood had covered the hatchet's handle, so there was no proof as to who had used it. Amy got away without any charges and the insurance company—avoiding any additional scandal—paid off without any delay on their policy. Within a few weeks, Amy was rich.

In the meantime, I nearly starved. Only by raiding the trash at night was I able to find anything to eat. I'd be well on my way to death by the time she ever left on a vacation. She was keeping her word. I never doubted that she would.

Occasionally, I'd find tidbits of food left under the sofa for me. Strange, through the scent of the food, I could smell Victor's odor. A couple of nights, I awoke to a scratching sound, but was too weak to investigate. Once I felt as if I were being petted by my old master, a wishful hallucination.

Then, about a month after Victor's murder, I woke to Amy screaming in the darkness. Her bedroom door was partially open, but I didn't want to use the energy to see what was happening. She wasn't worth the effort.

Awaking very late the next morning, I was surprised that she hadn't risen as usual. Too weak to take a chance on her catching me, I gave her until later that day before gathering up the courage to check it out. Though surprised at what I saw, I was extremely grateful.

After another week, her absence was beginning to be noticed by the neighbors. They'd left her alone to grieve, but not seeing her out, they were concerned as to her well-being. The postman, dealing with an overflowing mailbox, stopped by the police department, and asked if they'd check things out.

I recall my surprise as the door burst open. Their hollering "Is anyone in here" was only met with silence. I would have gotten up to greet them but had a full stomach from just having eaten and only wanted to sleep. That was going to be an impossibility.

I should have known things would get hectic once they entered her bedroom. Finding Amy's body had to be a shock. I'm not sure if finding Victor's rotting hand around her neck or part of her body having been eaten away shocked them more.

Yes, Victor had kept his promise. His practices of Black Magic had allowed a part of him to have its revenge on her. All those nights in the basement, chanting and practicing spells, had been worth it in the end.

And, I'd had my vengeance, too. Although she promised I'd starve, I'd found Amy to be mighty tasty, although a bit ripe during those final days. She had indeed fed me—maybe not as one would expect—but still, food is food.

After all, a girl's gotta eat. Right?

*****

I could think of only one thing to say, "That was kind of weak. You got anything better. Otherwise, I need to get back to my other project."

"Well, it wasn't my best one, but I thought you'd want to hear about my lives in chronological order. It was bad enough to send me to Hell to await being reborn. I guess eating flesh is frowned upon in Heaven."

"It would be worse if you were human," I responded, thinking how I could change the story to reflect that, but coming up with nothing. "How about a scary one that you heard in line while waiting for your next life? You know, something besides a cheating wife killing her husband plot?"

"Okay, you asked for it. I told a few friends this one and they couldn't sleep for days. Kept checking their beds for visitors…"

Snake, Rattle, and Roll

"Damn, one of these days someone will figure out a way to get water into the house without having to draw it up from a well and carry bucket after bucket."

"Don't let Mama hear you using that word, Daniel. She'll whip the tar out of you. I don't know what you're complaining about, anyway. I'm the one that has to carry it in all the way inside. You're just pulling up the buckets."

"Wait until you're big enough to do it, Joshua. You'll find out it's not as easy as you think. Carrying them buckets just builds up your muscles for when you have to pull them up filled with water."

At least the weather was cool. Fall had arrived a few weeks back and left the scorching days of Summer behind. Didn't have to worry as much about snakes, either. Most had found a den to survive the cold months. Pa checked out the barn and got rid of one or two that tried to nest there. That was before he'd headed off to war to fight the Rebels.

He was in charge of the farm now, well, except for Mama, and she'd taken ill of late, spending most of her time sleeping. It was up to him to see things got done and they all got fed, and he took his responsibility seriously. His thirteen years had been tough ones on the prairie. Not a lot of fun. He mostly helped his father maintain the sod house, plant a few crops, and take care of the livestock. Last year, he'd found he wasn't yet big enough to handle the plow and the horse team at the same time. Couldn't use that as an excuse next Spring. With Pa gone, there wasn't anyone else to do it.

Daniel watched as Joshua struggled to keep his balance toting the two buckets, once full of water. He hoped his younger brother wouldn't spill more than had already sloshed out along the way. Shaking his head, he tossed another bucket down into the well, jerked the rope around to let the bucket sink, and began pulling it up. *Two more buckets ought to do it.* With two already inside and the two Joshua carried, it would give them plenty for making dinner, washing up, and taking care of the supper dishes. He'd almost pulled the bucket to the top when he heard a scream.

"Daniel, help!" Joshua screamed. "I'm not kidding, help!"

"You better not be," hollered Daniel. Off and running, he saw his brother had almost made it to the house. He'd dropped both buckets and was standing still, staring at something between him and the sod home. Almost to Joshua's side, he spied the problem—three rattlers were coiled and ready to strike just a couple of feet from the young boy.

"Stand still," he ordered. "I'm going to the barn and get the hoe. If you move they'll bite, so don't twitch a muscle."

Working his way around Joshua, he noticed the closest one following his movements, while the others kept the young boy targeted. Once out of strike range, Daniel sprinted off. Reaching the barn door, he lifted the drop board out of its slot and pulled back. Scraping along the dirt, it slowly opened. He rushed in, grabbed a hoe, and turned to leave. A couple of yards ahead of him was the largest rattler he'd ever seen, crawling right toward him!

"Now, that don't make a lick of sense," he exclaimed. "Snakes don't crawl at people, they usually scoot away from them." He raised the hoe high above his head, aimed, and brought it down hard. He'd been fast, but the snake had been faster. It avoided the iron blade and pulled itself back. Raising its head high, it used its coils to inch backward to a pile of loose boards close to the door. The reptile then did something Daniel had never witnessed—it crawled in reverse and worked its way under the boards.

I'll be, it's almost like it knows I can't get to it there. Pa always said snakes couldn't crawl backward. Guess this one proved him wrong.

"Daniel!"

It was Joshua. Knowing he had to get to him, Daniel did his best to get out without getting bitten by the rattler hiding close by. The buzzing of its rattle hadn't stopped, but it had chosen a good hiding place. No matter how hard he searched to see it, the boards provided no observation. Reaching the doorway, he turned and bolted toward his brother, leaving the barn wide open.

Joshua still stood where he'd been left, but the snakes had grown bold and gotten well within a foot of his brother. Daniel moved forward, respecting the fact they could strike his brother any time they wanted, and tried to get their attention. He knew if he could get close enough, he might be able to use the hoe and pull them away. That would give Joshua a chance to run around them and get inside.

Slowly, he slid the hoe along the dirt toward the first. Raising its head above the top coil, it struck the iron blade with unbelievable speed. The other two joined the first and announced their anger at his intrusion, buzzing their rattles at top speed. Daniel raised the head of the hoe about six inches and brought it close to the same snake a second time. Again, it struck, but this time, Daniel dropped the blade, pinning the snake against the rough terrain. Jerking the hoe back, he dragged the serpent away from Joshua. Once clear, Daniel raised the blade and slammed it down several times, leaving the wounded animal writhing in pain. One final slice and the head was severed from its body. Only two more to go!

Yet, unlike their common behavior, one of the snakes kept its head aimed at Daniel and the one furthest away turned and eyed Joshua. The youngster turned away in fear and stepped back. The triangular head blurred forward as it shot itself at the target and sank its fangs into the young child's calf.

Daniel jumped forward and brought the hoe down on the second. Pushing Joshua out of further harm's way, he swung the hoe at the second, catching the snake in mid-strike and sending it yards in the other direction. Rushing to his brother, he took hold of his arm and yanked him to the house, keeping the hoe ready in case they came upon another rattler along the way.

Once inside, the door securely fastened shut, Daniel set Joshua on the table and pulled up his pant leg. Two dots of blood confirmed the fangs had made contact and injected their deadly venom. Grabbing a knife, Daniel made a deep slice over the marks and tried to suck out the venom.(1) Wrapping a clean rag around the wound, he lay Joshua upon his bed.

"You're gonna get real sick," he told the youngster. "And, your leg is gonna swell up big. But, I think you'll live. You gotta lay still, though. Otherwise, the poison will spread to the rest of your body."

Nodding through tears, Joshua took hold of his pillow and put it over his face. He'd been around long enough to know men didn't cry. Still, since he couldn't stop, he had to muffle his sobbing.

Brave young kid, Daniel thought, *I pray he makes it. That snake got him good. None of this makes any sense, though. First, the weather is too cold for the snakes to be out. Second, snakes don't gather like those three did unless they're around their den. If there was a den around, we'd have found more snakes around during the warmer weather. Third, that big one in the barn wasn't afraid of me at first. Snakes crawl away if you leave them alone, not at you. That one wanted to attack me. And, the way it had crawled backward—that just doesn't happen. Fourth, those three snakes seemed like they'd teamed up together. Snakes don't form packs or ever work together. Fact is, unless they're mating, you don't ever see more than one at a time. These three had positioned themselves strategically around Joshua, moved closer to him all at once, and while I went after one of them, another kept his eyes on me and the third attacked Joshua. It was like they each had a job to do. Nope, don't make any sense at all.*

"Daniel, what's going on? You were making a lot of noise a while ago." Finally awake, his mother had come out from behind the blanket hanging from the ceiling, making her bedroom in the one room dwelling. "What's Joshua doing in bed?"

"Rattler got him. I cut it and tried to suck out the poison. I think he's asleep. You might want to take a look at him."

"Why didn't you wake me? You know I am the adult around here," she replied.

"I took care of it. Thought it better to let you sleep. You ain't been right since Pa left. What's wrong with your leg? You're limping."

"Ain't figured it out, yet, she said looking up from Joshua's side. "Leg hurts like the devil, mouth tastes bad, and I'm pretty dizzy. Had a sweating spell a little while ago. May go back to bed. Looks like you took care of Joshua just fine. Ain't much more we can do right now."

"Let's look at it. You might have cut it on something and it's got infected."

Raising up her gown, Daniel saw some dried blood that had run down her leg. Higher up her thigh, swollen to twice its normal size, blood blisters circled a six-inch area of black skin. "Mama, this looks like a snake bite!"

"Can't be. I've been in bed all afternoon. It's been cold in here. Joshua kept leaving the door open when he brought in water.

Daniel hurried to the hoe he'd leaned against the wall and walked to his mother's bed. Using the hoe, he snagged the blankets and pulled them back. Coiled by the foot of the mattress was a two-foot rattler. Maneuvering the hoe handle under the snake, he lifted it off the bed. Dropping to the floor, it assumed strike position just in time to feel the blade slice it in half. Daniel picked up a bucket by the door and used the hoe blade to pick up the half with the head. Even cut in half, the mouth opened, and half inch fangs hit the iron, leaving a trail of venom behind. Setting the hoe aside, he picked up the bottom half by the rattle and dropped it in the bucket with the top half.

"Mama, we should bleed out that bite on your leg."

"No, I'll be okay," she replied, a strange tone to her voice. "I just need a little rest."

"Mama, you know better. That snake bite is a bad one. You could die."

"Look after your brother, Daniel. I need to lie down. I'm feeling poorly."

He kept trying to get her to let him bleed the bite area, but she ignored his request regardless of what he said. Daniel watched as she put her robe on the chair next to her bed and climbed back in. Within moments she was asleep. That's how the snake got into her bed. He entered when Joshua had left the door open and used the chair to climb up high enough to stretch over onto the mattress.

This is too strange, his mind repeated over and over. It was like the rattler planned an attack and carried through with it! What in the world was going on?

"Daniel, Daniel are you there?"

Joshua was moaning out his name. Sitting on the side of his cot, Daniel reached up to feel his forehead. He was burning up! Rushing to the table, he grabbed a towel off the back of a chair and dampened it in a wash tub of water. Laying it across Joshua's temple, he couldn't help but see the youngster, grimacing in pain.

"It hurts so bad, Daniel," he whispered, gritting his teeth. "So bad."

"You're gonna be okay. I promise, the pain won't go on much longer."

Joshua attempted a smile but scrunched up his face as another wave passed through his body. Daniel tried to hold his hand, but his brother's fingers were clenched, tight enough that the fingernails were cutting into his palm and drawing blood. His sweating had been replaced with shivering. Daniel pulled up the blanket and climbed into bed. Lying next to his brother, he realized that it was cold in the room. Glancing to the fireplace, he saw only dying embers.

Getting up to throw a log on, sparks scattered as something dropped into the ashes. It happened again, but this time, he saw what had caused the fireworks.

Two rattlers had fallen down the chimney!

Grabbing the hoe once more, he ran to the fireplace as both exited the ashes. Crawling at full speed toward him, the reptiles were on a mission—one that he couldn't let them succeed. Bringing the hoe down on the closest one, the reptile's life ended. Yet, the second one continued forward—too close to swing the weapon. Daniel sprang to his right and back several steps, changing direction before the snake could build an attack. He grabbed the tub of water as he slipped by the table and brought it down atop the snake. As it struggled to free itself from the weight of the tub, Daniel brought the blade down and the head separated from the body, flopping in a circle as it bit at the air.

Rushing to the fireplace, Daniel threw some dried corn husks on the embers. Within seconds they'd ignited. Tossing some wood chips atop the husks to get the fire blazing, he then added a couple of logs as a finally topping. Standing with his hoe, he kept guard until the fire was roaring, knowing anything that attempted to enter this way would now be roasted trying.

As darkness replaced the light of day, Daniel cut up a potato, added some smoked pork, and used the last bucket of water to make some soup. The fire was almost too high to cook over it, but a few minor burns and some patience proved to be a good price for the meal it made. Fixing a bowl for his mother, Daniel found her impossible to wake. The same held true with Joshua. Neither responded to his voice efforts, and when he shook their shoulders, both cried out in pain and begged to be left alone.

The fumes from the oil lamps, after a few hours, were suffocating. Plus, the fireplace flue didn't seem to be working properly. A lot of smoke was coming back into the room. Daniel worked the lever, but it would only partially move. Waiting until the fire died down some, he picked up the iron rod they used to unclog it and stuck it up the chimney. He hit something soft and used the rod to work it loose. Into the fire fell the bodies of several rattlers, burnt to a crisp. Quickly, he grabbed another log and threw it on the fire and returned to his watch post to ensure no live serpents followed the others down.

As night continued, Daniel's breathing grew more difficult. Fresh air wasn't just wished for, it was becoming his only option to dying from the poisonous fumes. Surely, with the lower temperatures, the snakes outside would be too cold to move, let alone try to attack. He placed his hand on the one window they had. Cold, not enough to frost, but close. There was no way the snakes could be active.

Not knowing what to expect the next morning, Daniel put on his jacket, grabbed the hoe, and latched hold of the handles of two buckets. He figured it would be a good time to go to the well and get some water for the next day without having to worry about snakes. He turned, making sure the fire was going strong, and then opened the door.

The buckets fell from his hand. In the doorway was a three-foot-high pile of rattlers. The ones that had been against the door had stayed warm by the door's warmth, as well as being insulated from the cold by the others exposed to the elements. Working their way free of the pile, several crossed the door sill and entered before Daniel could get the door shut. The house was under attack!

Wildly swinging, the boy got two of them with one hit. Their side by side entrance, meant to overwhelm, provided an easy target. Four others, splitting in different directions, made Daniel's task of protecting his family much more difficult. Taking another swing, he took out one that had made biting Daniel its goal. Another died as it sped around him vying for a rear attack.

The boy rushed over to the bed Joshua was lying upon and barely saved his brother from being bitten again as the snake wrapped its body around a bedpost and climbed up. Daniel spun around in time to see the rattle of the last disappear under the hanging blanket that provided his mother privacy from the boys. Rushing over, he was shocked to see that the speed of the rattler had already placed it on her pillow. Before he could stop it, its fangs penetrated the side of her neck once, and then a second. In rage, the boy hooked it with the hoe and repeatedly separated parts of its body with the blade, returning the brutality of the reptile's attack.

Walking to his mother's side, he saw her lying still. Daniel touched her cheek and found it cold and hard. The snake's attack had been for nothing. She'd obviously been dead for quite some time. He covered her head with the blanket that had once been used to keep her warm. Her body would never be that way again.

Perhaps, if it had been a normal evening, he would have allowed himself a period to grieve. Forcing himself to ignore the emotional wave that was working to engulf him, he wiped his eyes and walked over to his brother's side. He deposited the snake there into a bucket, now almost full of dead reptiles. He checked the rag he'd laid on Joshua's forehead earlier and found it dry. Placing his hand upon his brother's cheeks to see if the fever had returned, he discovered it to be as cold as his mother's. Another blanket raised to cover a dead family member.

He left his brother and returned to the chair at the fireplace. Lost in thought, Daniel stared into the flames as his mind flew through the day. It had been normal, as any other, until the incident with the rattlers. None of that made any sense. Snakes acted upon instinct. Their brains were too tiny to do anything else. Yet, these had formed themselves into a fighting unit, he imagined much like the one his Pa had joined to fight in the war. Their actions served a purpose, of which he was unsure. The only thing he was sure of was that his brother and mama were dead, and that he was alone, miles from the closest neighbor. It was too much for his young brain to handle. He broke down and let his emotions flow.

Sometime during the night, he'd cut off all but one oil lamp to reduce the fumes. There was no way he intended to open the front door and watch more snakes rush inside. The warmth of the fireplace soon took over and sent him into the world of dreams, and nightmares.

He saw himself and Joshua playing outside, chasing each other around, as the sun settled in the West. Both laughing and wearing huge grins, they hadn't a care in the world. Their pa was coming in from the fields and Mama was fixing an evening meal that smelled so good people's mouths in the next county were watering. The two boys wrestled on the ground for a minute, but Daniel turned it into a tickling match and showed no mercy on Joshua, who kept proclaiming, "I gotta pee, I gotta pee" between fits of uncontrollable laughter.

Then, a shadow came over them and a giant rattlesnake used his coils to cave in the house atop Mama. It then shot out and swallowed Pa in one bite. It was coming for the two boys, its black eyes turning demon red and blazing more and more the closer it got. It struck, grabbing Joshua, but missing Daniel as he rolled off to the side. It coiled back into strike position, its rattle sounding like a thousand locusts invading the prairie. Its tongue flickered as it savored the smell of fear within its prey. Daniel had run out of options. He was the target, the prize, the winner's trophy.

The giant struck—Daniel rolled aside to escape the attack—and fell out of his chair. Gathering his senses, he shivered as the chill of a sweat soaked shirt sent goosebumps up and down his back. The sun of a new day was beaming in through the window, warming that which sat in its rays. Yet, the room was cold. He turned to see the fire had died. He rushed to get it going, fearing a rattlesnake would drop from above any second, if it hadn't already done so during his slumber.

Searching the room from his chair, his mind and eyes played tricks and the shadows began to move. He picked up the hoe and beat the visions of serpents gliding around the corner and slice the demons sliding through the stucco walls. Yet, no blood did it draw.

He walked to the window and focused on the dirt and weeds next to the house. No movement and no snakes—just strong wind stirring up dust. Fifty yards away a couple of prairie dogs were nibbling on some brambles and keeping a lookout for insects. Everything looked like just another morning.

Should he open the door or not? The water was gone. In his panicked search for serpents, he'd knocked over the bucket holding the little that had remained. Thirst wasn't an issue yet, but it soon would be. Plus, the livestock in the barn needed food and water. He couldn't ignore them. They might be able to go a day or two, but sooner or later, he'd have to tend to them.

Placing his shoe less than half an inch from the door's edge, he released the latch. The force of the outside wind took hold of the door and pushed it against Daniel's foot. It didn't budge. With greatest care, he slid his foot back in quarter in increments until he could see the front of the door sill through the crack. There were no snakes—only the pebbles and stones he and his brother had gathered to make a walkway to the house.

He continued inching open the door until he had a clear view of the yard. Nothing. Reaching down, he picked up two buckets by their handles and grabbed the hoe in the other. Step by step, he moved cautiously to the well. After filling the two buckets, he picked them up to start his trip back, the hoe clenched in his armpit. On his second step, a rattle sounded.

To his left, a small prairie rattler sat coiled and ready to strike. Giving it wide berth, he slowly proceeded, only to find another blocking his path back to the house, and then another, and another. They had formed a border he couldn't cross, one that led straight to the barn. He attempted to retrace his steps but discovered the ones he'd passed had fallen in behind—eliminating that option—and were moving forward.

The closer Daniel got to the barn, the more rattlers lined his route. Veering too close to one side or the other, brought a warning strike, sometimes too close as the serpent's snout would bounce against his leg. It was if he was running a gauntlet, but one aimed at herding instead of injuring. They wanted him in the barn, that was clear. He had no choice. Whatever awaited him would have to be dealt with when he got inside.

The barn door was still open from the night before, when Joshua had first hollered for his help. The thought of his brother sent his emotions running wild. Love was replaced with sorrow, and then anger. Although his mama had taught vengeance is the Lord's, somehow, he'd find a way to get even first—or die trying.

Tentative, Daniel stepped inside, jumping away from the pile of boards where the large rattler hid yesterday. The hogs and cows were restless in their stalls, hungry and thirsty he bet.

Still carrying the buckets of water, he decided to pour them in the animals' troughs. Leery of putting himself in a good spot to be attacked, he kept a keen eye on his surroundings. After dividing the water among the livestock the best he could, Daniel opened the rear doors of each stall to allow the animals a chance to escape. None of the snakes had entered from the front during his time inside, none that he'd seen at least. Skeptical of that continuing, he decided the center of the barn floor would be the best position to man a defense.

Minutes crept by. Daniel had to keep turning to keep from being ambushed from the sides or rear. The rising temperature invigorated his captors, slithering among themselves, and never leaving the positions they held by the front door.

Daniel had stopped trying to figure the whole thing out. It didn't matter what or who was controlling them. Maybe it was an act of the Devil—maybe God. Mama and Joshua were dead. He would probably follow. There were too many for him if they all attacked at once. A solitary bite would do the job. Anything more would simply be overkill. Either way, he didn't look forward to it. One thing for sure, he'd go down fighting, killing as many as he could!

A strong gust of wind slammed the front door shut. A cow bellowed out and Daniel jerked around to see if it had been attacked. Beside him, a long, thick body dropped where his shoulder had been seconds before. It was the huge rattler he'd tried to kill yesterday!

Daniel leapt back, narrowly escaping the venom filled fangs of the striking monster. Instead of coiling up, it serpentined with tremendous speed, it's body barely avoiding the hoe's iron blade. The snake shifted directions faster than Daniel could swing, all the time getting closer to the boy.

His shoulders ached and his fingers throbbed from the repeated impacts of the hoe against the stones that covered the barn floor. But, he couldn't stop. This snake had chosen a surprise attack and had failed. Now, he planned on the element of surprise shifting.

Maneuvering the attack back to the stall area, the snake followed with untold aggression. Success of strikes no longer concerned the animal as it pursued the target. Blinded by its madness, the triangular head shot out over and over, sometimes missing by feet, other times by inches. Its rattle echoed the ferocity and desperation to sink its fangs into the young flesh ahead. The rattler wasn't frightened of the boy's larger size as others of its kind were. Aware it's bite held the messenger of death, bravery wasn't an issue.

Daniel circled away from the stacked barrels and sacks of grain as the snake reached them. The snake struck out as the boy chopped down with the hoe. Daniel's swing hit the grain bag to which it had been aimed and lodged itself deep inside. Yanking back with all his strength, the bag fell off the wooden barrel and atop the squirming serpent, pinning it to the floor. It desperately tried to free itself, but the iron blade fell too soon. Once the attacker, the large serpent found freedom from the grain bag, as only its bottom half lie beneath. Determined to kill, the snake tried to continue the attack, but only wobbled from side to side, unable to use its coil to push forward any longer. Another swing and the head was split from snout to neck, it's brain destroyed.

The sound of vibrating rattles outside the front door ceased, leaving only the sound of the wind droning around the building.

Daniel dropped the hoe and stared at the body on the floor. He had no questions as to why, only a sense of relief. Two warriors had fought to the death. One lie dead. The battle was over.

He walked over to the wall and took down a bridle. Walking out the back door, he whistled loudly, then again. A plow horse trotted to meet the boy and gave no resistance to the bridle Daniel pulled over his head. After leading the horse to a wooden fence, the boy climbed to the second rail and mounted the bare back. Jabbing his heels into the horse's ribs, the two faced the wind and trotted across the prairie.

Daniel was familiar with the way to the closest neighbors. He'd traveled there with his pa many times. They were friendly, God fearing people, always willing to share with a neighbor. He knew they'd help him if they could.

His leg throbbed and had begun to swell. The fangs had delivered their venom just before the grain bag fell atop the snake. Perhaps, the neighbors knew of some remedy that he didn't to keep him alive. If not, he would soon be with Mama and Joshua. They hadn't heard from Pa since he'd left for the Yankee Army. He'd never thought of it before, but maybe he had been killed in battle. Mama had received a letter that looked official but had never shared its contents. She hadn't been the same since.

A dizzy feeling was setting in as Daniel spied the neighbor's sod house as he rode over the rise. A huge amount of smoke billowed out of its chimney. *Funny, it's not that cold a day. What could cause them to have that big of a fire going?*

* * * * *

(1) Note: The method of treating snakebite used in the previous story is no longer an acceptable method. Please consult the medical information available concerning snakebite treatment in your area of residency for proper methodology.

* * * * *

"Like that one?"

"I have to say, it was much better than the first one you told. You know I hate snakes, don't you?"

"Most people do." Gabriela grinned and licked her paws. "I find them interesting creatures. They're really kind of beautiful and they get a bad rap most of the time. Kind of like black cats. And, I'm an expert on that."

"So, what's up next … something just as good or even better?"

"I think I'll tell you about my second life. It's better than the first for your purpose of entertaining the readers. Ready to go to the mountains?"

Big Feet Minus Expensive Shoes

Back in the 1960's, I lived with a man named Bobby Howard in the hill country of Eastern Kentucky. Bobby wasn't a bad person but let us say he wasn't the most intelligent of all my owners. Today, we would call him a hillbilly. Back then, he called himself a God-fearing common man. For all his faults, he did attend church every Sunday. Afterward, Bobby would stop the old pick-up about five-hundred yards down the road and sell his moonshine out of the back. You might say he loved spreading the Holy Spirit as well as the spirits of the still.

Bobby lived in an old shack that had sheltered his kin for almost a century. Rotten shutters missing hinges hung awkwardly, the roof leaked into pots and pans each time it rained, and broken boards all over the porch made walking a hazard. So weathered was the exterior that a coat of paint wouldn't have helped much, so my owner didn't bother. He'd found the benefit of sheet tin and how simple it was to slap a sheet over a rotting section of the wall. This kept out most of the cold winter winds and could be pulled off to admit cooling breezes during the summer.

I spent most of my time in the barn where the mice thrived. Between the grain spilled on the floor around the cattle feeders and the slop that sloshed out of the trough for the pigs, the mice filled their tummies and grew nice and fat. I never had to look far for a meal and had to eat in moderation to keep my figure. Nothing worse than a bunch of chubby, laughing mice scurrying away because one is too fat to chase them. I can still hear Bobby's voice warning me, "Girl, iffin' you get any fatter, the mice are gonna catch you and have barbecued cat for their dinner." Like I said, not my most intelligent owner, but his point was well taken.

One late fall evening—after a particularly wonderful meal of the fattest two mice I'd ever seen—I was snuggled up between bales of hay in the barn loft keeping nice and warm. Through the cracks in the side of the building, I was mesmerized by the flickering of the fireplace flames inside his home across the barn lot. The flames, dancing in the shadows, looked so alive. So hypnotic were they that I couldn't take my eyes away. A slight breeze through that same crack brought in the sweetest smoke my nose ever had the pleasure of inhaling, if inhaling smoke is one's thing.

Behind me, the rustling about of mice pulled me from my dreamlike state. Not just one or two were moving about, but all that resided on the far side of the building were stampeding across the floor—heading in my direction! Remembering my master's warning, I readied myself for an attack. I wasn't going to end up as an all you can eat buffet. If they were massing to make a purge; I would be ready. I eased out of my warm, comfortable bed to face the onslaught—claws extended.

Onward they came—the sound of hundreds of little feet running up the ladder. I had faith I could withstand an attack of ten, maybe even twenty of them—not the mouse population of six counties, though. I searched around for a position they'd have a hard time reaching to make their attack on me. Sadly, I accepted the fact that I was in as good as place as any. If it came down to it, I could always jump down and escape from the barn to the forest close by. But, before it came to that, I'd make sure to kill a few for principle.

It was then my nostrils noticed a mixture of the smell of rotten potatoes, skunk scent, and roadkill odors from outside. Horrible as the smell was, my attention perked to the deep grunting—guttural noises—that accompanied the stench.

The mice and I lined the loft rafter beam, all seeking to know what the source of this disturbance was. Most of the rodents were perched on their back legs, ready to scatter at the first hint of impending danger. Yet, curiosity's hold kept them from finding safe hiding. Somewhat expected—me being the supposed "curious one"—it was doing the same to me.

Thousands of muscles tensed as the small entry door banged open. Many observers backed away from the beam's edge—ready to get a head start if hiding became a necessity. Waiting on what was to appear became more than just a curiosity—it was potentially a matter of life and death.

It was then a gigantic, hairy manlike creature squeezed through sideways, barely making it inside. It stood tall and straight in the moonlight—its head almost as high as the rafter upon which we sat. The creature sniffed the various smells of the barn and its occupants—somehow able to distinguish them from its own pungency—before suddenly hopping at us watching.

Wasting no time, I returned to my hiding spot between the hay bales, along with twenty or thirty of the mice that had been nearby. Multiple grunts in quick succession followed. *Damn, it's laughing at us! That damn thing scared us just to play around.*

Not entirely certain of my analysis, I crept out, cautious of my bravery and curiosity landing me in trouble. Peering from over the edge, I watched the beast stroll over to the hog stall and snag one of the newly born piglets. The high-pitched squeals of its prey ended quickly with a head twisting and a neck snapping. Not satisfied with one, the beast grabbed another and repeated his actions. Backing the remaining three babies against the outside wall, the mother faced off against the ruthless monster—warning snorts threatening a forthcoming battle should it decide to attempt another murder. She'd been caught by surprise and shock as the first two had been taken from her and wouldn't allow a third without a fight.

Fifty yards away, the front door slammed shut against its door frame. Running footsteps neared and the barrel of a shotgun nosed inside. Seizing the two dead piglets by their hind legs in one of his humongous hands, the beast covered the distance to the door in three huge strides. I sat stunned as the monster grabbed hold of the shotgun's barrel and yanked it from Bobby's hands. Tossing it aside, he roared, defying my owner to face him barehanded. God-fearin' Bobby, showing all the intelligence I failed to give him credit for, turned and skedaddled back to the house.

Watching until my owner was behind the closed door, he let out a series of quick grunts. He stood tall, seemingly proud, and somewhat amused at his results. Walking over to where the shotgun lay, he examined it with interest before bending the barrel into a half circle. Giving us a parting glance, he raised his hand as if to wave before picking up the two dead piglets and exiting into the night.

In less than five minutes, the creature had succeeded in procuring food and scaring every living animal and human present. Now, that's the way to make a statement!

Amazed and excited at what I'd witnessed—and having no desire in wasting an opportunity—I grabbed a quick bedtime snack of the closest mouse and lay back between the hay bales. My head, full of the sights of the event, recalled a conversation in Hell with another feline. He had described an elusive beast not unlike the one here. It had been called a "Bigfoot" by him, which obviously applied. My acquaintance had expressed relief at having been able to escape the creature's wrath, only to be hit by a car a week later while chasing a small field mouse. I felt much the same.

The next morning—while dreaming of a Siamese fantasy lover with the most gorgeous green eyes—I was stirred from my delights by the voices of my owner and many more of his kind.

"Damn thing was a monster, bigger than anything I've ever seen," Bobby told the others gathered. "It roared so loud I thought my ears were gonna bust wide open. Grabbed my gun away, like it knew what I'd planned on doin', and was ready to tear me apart. I barely escaped with my life!"

"Now, Bobby, might you not be telling us a tale? After all, you said you'd just woke up to the pigs squealing," one of the men offered while trying to hide a grin. "Ain't never seen nothin' like you describe. Could it have been a bear, instead?"

"Wasn't no bear," my owner spat out, frowning at the suggestion. "You think I'm crazy, do you? Let me show you the tracks I found. You'll see for yourselves, wasn't no damn bear. Looks like a barefoot giant's footprint, I swear!"

As Bobby headed the men toward his evidence, I thought back a few hours and of the Bigfoot creature. It did look like a hairy giant and nothing like a bear. The beast had displayed skills in stealth, thievery, and killing, much like many in the animal kingdom. Yet, bravery, calculating intelligence, and even humor made it humanlike. Bigfoot was indeed a creature of profound uniqueness.

I passed on breakfast—my midnight snack still lying heavy in my stomach—and joined Bobby and the men. Disbelief covered the faces of most of the men as Bobby presented them the footprints he'd found. Hoping to help, I strolled over beside one of the impressions, dropped to the ground, and stretched out. Able to compare, many of the disbelievers gasped seeing the footprint was much longer. And, I'm no small kitty!

Hunting dogs, barking in the back of the men's trucks, reminded me to return to the barn before I became part of the canine breakfast menu. There, I watched as all gathered their weapons and dogs and headed off into the woods. The baying of the hounds on a scent trail faded after a few minutes. All the activity had brought around my appetite, so I grabbed a small mouse for my own breakfast and took a nap.

Between the excitement of the previous night and my early awakening, I must have been more tired than I'd imagined. The sun fading over the horizon greeted me as I awoke. Exiting the barn,

I relieved myself under one of the pick-up trucks still sitting in the barn lot. The lateness of the day made me wonder where all the men were. Even during hunting season, they would have returned by this time of day. Of course, humans are not the most predictable creatures, but this was odd even for them. From the barn, group of snorting, hungry hogs and mooing cattle wondered the same.

Famished, I partook of my evening meal and headed to the loft. Cleaning myself off, I heard footsteps running from the woods. Hoping to see Bobby—more for the sake of the penned-up livestock than myself—I hopped down to greet him.

Instead of Bobby, one of the others came into view. His face was filled with fear as he headed towards his truck. Panting with exhaustion, he turned and emptied his rifle into the forest before digging in his pocket for his keys. Before he could open the door, a nine-feet-tall monster burst from the woods and pulled him away. The man's legs wagged in mid-air as the Bigfoot held him high with one arm, roaring in his face. *I guess he didn't like being shot at.*

The beast's other hand covered the top of the man's head and twisted, duplicating the crackling sound of the piglets' necks, and silencing the hunter's screams of agony. Not stopping there, he continued to rotate the head until the flesh and bones could take no more, ripping it from the man's body. Dropping the lifeless parts, the beast let loose with a series of loud, but short roars. I guessed it to be a victory announcement. How wrong I was.

In seconds, nine more of the beasts appeared, their heights varying between five to eight feet. Like a pillaging horde, the group raided the barn of livestock--killing the poultry and pigs--and herding the larger cattle into the forest. Barking out commands, the largest directed the plundering with efficiency, as if this wasn't the first farm they'd raided. Soon, only the mice and I remained alive, watching as the last of them disappeared into the underbrush.

Curious, I followed using their scent to guide me. It was a simple task—them stinking as they did—and soon I was deeper in the woods than I'd ever been. Sidestepping the strike of a Timber Rattler, I barely escaped its fangs. Straying from the path had its dangers, but so did being easily seen. I proceeded with caution, lurking in the brush at every opportunity. Within a few minutes, I picked up the familiar grunts of the beasts. I took to the brush and crept forward, hoping to remain undiscovered ... and alive!

A few more feet forward presented me with over a dozen of the Bigfoot creatures working together in a clearing next to a bare rock wall. Young and old were busy stripping the meat from the bones of the livestock, now lying motionless on bloody beds of leaves. Many gorged themselves on their sinewy, bounty treats while others wrapped up the extra in the hides they had skinned from the bodies. The smallest, which I calculated to be the youngest, played a role by digging deep holes into the rocky soil. Others, a little larger, searched the area gathering the evidence of their butchery—bones and such—and burying all in these same holes.

What amazed me most was the blazing fire next to the rock wall. No animal could create fire. Yet, these creatures had done exactly that. In addition, they knew enough to know exactly what to burn—the clothes of those humans killed. I recognized several of the shirt patterns of those that had left our farm early that day, including that of Bobby's. They'd even sent a creature back to bring the body of the last one killed. His clothes joined the others in the flame as his skeleton was stripped of flesh. Obviously, these creatures weren't picky eaters, if it was meat they consumed.

I stayed hidden for hours, watching the creatures communicate and complete their tasks. Ashes from the fire were scattered and all remaining shreds of clothing, bone splinters, and bloody leaves were buried and covered with clean leaves. When finished, the area showed no hint of the creatures having ever been present, nor of their crimes.

The darkness of night arriving, the largest made a final inspection tour of the area ensuring no traces remained. Again, barking out orders, the group formed a single file line. Walking in the footsteps of the one they followed, they marched into the forest, the last, the eight-foot-tall one that I'd seen the night before, turning to give me a wave before heading out of sight.

It all made sense to me. The strange disappearances of hikers and families from their homes, farm animals, even family pets, all could be associated with these creatures. Elusive? Of course, they were. While Bigfoot hunters searched areas in which they'd been, the creatures traveled to another. They were nomadic, never staying too long in one spot. They buried all evidence of their kills, and probably did the same to those of their group that passed away due to accident or normal death. Unless someone was to strip away the surface of entire forest floors the world over, they'd never find proof these creatures existed.

Alone, the sadness of Bobby's death set in. He hadn't been a bad owner, nothing like Amy had been, and now there would be no human in my life. But, there was nothing I could do about it. So, I retraced my steps—being especially aware of the night hunting rattlers, foxes, and bobcats—and returned to the barn.

For over a year, I was able to thrive on the mice that chewed their way into the barrels of grain and the fresh spring behind the barn gave me plenty of water to drink. Unfortunately, it froze up in the cold months, making my thirst unbearable at times.

Most of the pick-up trucks were towed away early on, leaving only my owner's to rust away.

The roof of the house collapsed, crushing all inside. Soon, the remains were covered with wild plants as Mother Nature reclaimed the land as her own.

The vicious attack would never be forgotten. Many nights I would wake and listen for their approaching grunts and sniff the air for their stench. It was terrible stress—a recurring nightmare—one that shortened my life and turned my black whiskers white before their time.

And, even as I tell you this story, I sit here, worried about who these creatures are killing tonight. I've heard several families in the area are missing. I wonder…

* * * * *

"For a moment I thought you were going to get corny and say something like, "What's that noise at the back door?"

"No, that would be beneath my standards," Gabriela hissed back, obviously pissed at my comment. "No need to embellish when you're speaking the truth."

"So, Bigfoots do exist. Or, is the correct term Bigfeets?"

She almost smiled. "Now, who's getting corny?"

"Okay, you got me. That was bad. Seriously, do the Bigfoot creatures exist? I always thought they were myths."

"That's what they want you to believe. It's easier for them to remain hidden and catch victims unaware. By the way, what's that noise at the back door?"

"You really didn't go there, did you?"

"I couldn't resist. Here's a story you might find a little easier to believe."

The Devil's Gift

Blood sprayed from the exploding chest, soaking the five-year-old and her aunt's white bedspread. The body fell forward, crushing her deep into the mattress, its weight forcing her to feel the guts—still warm--slide against her bare torso. It was there she lay when her aunt returned home and discovered the gruesome scene. The woman ran from the house, leaving the girl still trapped, forcing herself to close her eyes and pray for someone to free her.

"Oh, shit … what in the hell happened here? Look, there's a girl under his body. Her leg is moving! Help me get her out."

Her eyes opened as a strange man and woman worked to shove her uncle's body aside and pull her out. They rushed her to the bathroom, washing her off and wrapping her in a full-size towel. She watched the police rush into the home, anxious to investigate the crime, only to hurry to the bathroom to release their late lunches in the commode. Wary looks in her direction were combined with a fear of the unknown as the violent nature of the uncle's death remained undetermined. She closed her eyes, hoping to forget what had happened, scared of what she had done and the punishment that would come her way. Curling up in the corner of the couch, she allowed herself to drift into a land where the people wore smiles, and no one thought of attacking another. Soon, she fell into a deep sleep. A sleep that would allow her to forget what had taken place—for years to come.

* * * * *

"What do you mean my alarm is going off?"

"Yes, ma'am, your home alarm has been triggered and has shown movement in the home," the voice on the phone responded. "We wanted to alert you in case you'd triggered it accidentally."

"I'm forty miles away and heading toward Indianapolis. Call the police, now!"

Just what I need, a damn burglar. Oh, God, what if they're vandals? The whole house will be destroyed by the time the police arrive—they're always so fast to respond these days—like following a fat woman in flip-flops with three kids pushing a cart down a supermarket aisle. I need to turnaround, fast.

Slamming on the brakes, Catherine cut the wheel and barely managed to skid into the "Authorized Vehicles Only" interstate crossing. "Yeah, I love you, too," she yelled out as the driver of the car following her flipped up his middle finger and blasted his horn. Nothing coming, she spun tires and spewed gravel as she whipped out into the closest southbound lane.

Gotta get home. Can't depend on the cops to stop anyone. Will the house be a mess? What will they steal? Will they hurt my little dog? No, they can't hurt him—I just got him a couple of weeks ago. I swear if they do anything to Peanut Butter, I'll...

Thoughts poured through her head faster than the speedometer could hit eighty-five. *He's such a sweet little thing for a Pekingese—wouldn't hurt a fly.* Horrible images of teenage ruffians beating her sweet Peanut Butter took the place of the road in front of her. She'd seen videos on social media of kids thinking it funny and laughing as they stepped on puppies with spiked heels, mimicking their yelps and giggling as ribs and spines splintered. Some had shown demented youngsters grabbing hold of the poor animal's legs and yanking them until muscles and cartilage ripped, leaving the animals unable to do anything but roll about in anguish. *How cruel and appalling. I swear, if anything like that happens to Peanut Butter, you better be sure to not let me find you. I'll do the same damn thing to you!*

"Move, damn it," hollering at a slow-moving eighteen-wheeler blocking the fast lane as it crawled past a slower one. "I don't have time to waste on your slow ass. Move!"

Fed up with the driver's insolence, Catherine whipped the SUV over to the right onto the road's shoulder. Accelerator punched to the floorboard, the vehicle lurched forward, passing the semi-trucks on the right, and jumping in front of them within seconds. Horns blared behind her from both trucks. *Yeah, it was dangerous, I know. But if your slow-moving asses hadn't had been in the way I wouldn't have had to do it.*

Glancing up, the trucks were only dots in the background in her rearview mirror. Whizzing past cars, the SUV dared any to block its progress. At ninety mph, the number of cars increased as she got closer to her hometown. Weaving in and out of traffic, Catherine pictured her dog lying dead in a pool of blood in the middle of the living room floor. Teenagers, laughing and joking, spray painting graffiti on her walls and shattering her glassware. All she and her husband had worked for would be gone or broken. *Why in the hell did you leave me, Jim? Why? We struggled for twenty-eight years. Then, when the kids were off and married, you looked at me and said, "Time for me to go." Off you went, like nothing we'd been through mattered. You cast it all aside. The last eight years have been hell. I got a job and paid off the house and did the things you should be doing--painting, feeding the cows and pigs, running the farm--man stuff. You left me, you bastard ... you left me. Now, everything's going to be ruined and little Peanut Butter is going to be dead. You son-of-a-bitch, it's all your fault!*

The blaring of a siren and blue lights flashing in the mirrors broke her concentration. Slowing down and pulling over, she grew more frustrated waiting for the officer to approach. *Will you hurry up and get your butt out of the car. I've got to get home. Maybe I can talk you into giving me an escort. Naw, that's never going to happen.*

"Ma'am, I need to see your license and proof of insurance."

"Officer, that's no problem," handing them to him. "But, can we hurry? I just got a call from the security company. My house has been broken into and I'm desperately trying to get home before something happens to my dog. I'm so afraid the burglars will hurt him and destroy everything I own. You can call CBA Security or the Mt. Johnson police. They'll verify it. I really need to get going."

"Do you realize how fast you were going through town? You were doing over eighty in a fifty-five zone. By all rights, I should take you to jail for reckless driving and endangerment."

"Officer, check out what I told you. I know I was driving fast, but there's a reason. This is an emergency!"

"I'll check it out, ma'am. Just stay in your car and I'll be back in a few minutes."

You better be, you bastard. I need to get to my Peanut Butter! I don't have time for you to play around on your radio and computer. My dog needs me!

The next nine minutes took forever to pass. Catherine, tempted to forget about the cop and head down the road, pulled her fingers from the key several times. *I think of the most stupid stuff when I'm supposed to be patient. Just like when I was young. Mom and Dad could never keep me from finding out where they hid the Christmas presents. Jim used to get so aggravated when I'd nag him about getting things done. There was no need to procrastinate, but he was the king of it. He had faults, too. He should have accepted mine.*

"Okay, we need to discuss several things," the officer started out after returning to her window. "First, I'm only going to give you a warning this time, but I've alerted the state police to be on the lookout for you. If they catch you doing one mph over the limit, you're going to jail. Second, your story checked out. The Mt. Johnson police are waiting at your house. Your dog is fine and so is the house. It's their guess that when the front door opened, and the alarm went off, the intruder was scared off. You'll need to verify that nothing was stolen once you got there. Be careful and don't let me catch you speeding ever again!"

"You won't, officer, I guarantee it," taking her I.D.'s from the officer and dropping them into the passenger's seat. Taking her time, Catherine pulled into her driveway twenty minutes later and saw the officer sitting on her porch. Waiting for her to walk over, he spoke out, "I've already searched the house for intruders. No one around. Why don't you look and see if you have anything missing?"

Opening the front door, Peanut Butter jumped up and ran to her arms. "My baby, I'm so glad you're okay. Momma was so worried about you."

Giving each room a quick once over, Catherine couldn't see that anything was out of place. If the thief had come in, they hadn't moved one item out of its assigned spot. Satisfied all was well, the officer drove off.

*****

The Chow didn't like her. Walking home from school each day, the animal would push its weight against the rickety fence, desperately attempting to reach its prey. Even when she'd walk on the opposite side of the street, its snarls and barks followed her until she was able to escape into her house.

Her foster parents had contacted the owner weeks before, but nothing had changed. The dog was a friendly pet, vicious to no one that didn't tease it—to hear them tell it. If the girl would leave it alone then it would leave her alone. No need to change a thing.

The dog's constant pushing against the rotten pickets worked several of the nails loose. It charged across the street toward her, wanting to maim or kill the one there. Suddenly, its head jerked back, halting its attack. The dog rose high upon its rear legs, the front being lifted by some unseen force. The mouth, filled with the teeth it would use to commit its savage act, opened wide, straining the muscles and ligaments with unspeakable pain until they popped, rendering them useless. The animal lay in the street choking from the blood it inhaled with every breath.

The police arrived at her house later but left quickly. She showed no signs of an attack and wasn't big enough to have done that type of injury to the dog. One officer remembered her uncle's death as they drove away. *That girl seems to have a habit of being around strange and violent events—ones without viable answers. There's something weird about her.*

* * * * *

"I didn't think he'd ever leave."

Catherine's stomach jumped to her throat. Turning, she saw a fellow church member's daughter. "You're Fred Hamilton's girl, aren't you?"

"Yeah, I'm Heather, the bad one of the bunch. I took off a few years ago and just got back. Been a while since I saw you. You're still as ugly as I remember. You got a lot of nice stuff. Not much that can be hocked, though. When you gonna get a decent television, anyway?"

"You've really grown up since I saw you last. What are you now, twenty-seven or twenty-eight? We went over the whole house—where were you hiding? And, Peanut Butter wasn't barking ... why?"

"Cops are such dummies. You've got all those empty boxes from online shopping stacked in the basement. I arranged a few and sat down in the middle with one over me. He walked right by me without even glancing over. The dog? No big deal. I always carry pet treats when I rob a place. Makes me a friend and keeps them quiet. Dogs are like men—feed 'em and they're happy."

"Got it all figured out, don't you? So, what now? You know I can identify you."

"You're gonna die, that's what," the girl replied without a hint of emotion. "I can't have you blabbing to everyone, so, there's really not much choice, is there?"

Catherine stared at Heather. *I can take this girl. She's small so she can't be that strong.*

"Oh, by the way, go ahead and turn around. Let me introduce you to Jackie. People tend to die around her. She likes to stick them with knives and lick the blood off the blade. It's a fetish she has. Kind of turns me on to watch her do it. She was hiding between the quilts you have on that monster display rack in the spare room. Like I said, that cop was a real dumbass."

A tall, muscular woman comically bowed, her outstretched hand loosely holding a fisherman's skinning knife with an eight-inch blade. The chromed steel tilted, catching the sun's rays through the window and reflecting a glint in her eyes.

* * * * *

There were those who were wary of her quiet manner and those who openly teased her. She didn't fit in with the popular clique in high school, but her new foster parents had too much money to be a part of the other crowds. Devoting herself to her studies only separated her more from the norm.

She'd been surprised when a boy had asked her out. Even more surprised when he'd taken her to an out of the way forest spot and parked the car, expecting more than she was willing to give. She left him there, cooling her temper during the long walk home. She had controlled herself and was proud.

School turned into a nightmare for her the next week. Comments, like "I hear you're a great lay" and "C'mon baby, give me some of what you gave him" flooded her ears from the guys. The girls were as bad, presenting her looks and more slurs that shamed her.

After school, she sought out the boy that had spread the lies and found him riding a mower along a steep bank. The speed in which it flipped sideways and rolled over him was only surpassed by his instant dive into the spinning blades. Rolling in the grass, his arms, now stubs, shot blood wherever he aimed until the pressure slowed it to a weak flow.

Again, she was questioned, but witnesses had already stated she was far from the accident and couldn't have caused it. The officer on the scene had his doubts but had no way of proving it. He heard she was later taken in by another foster family. He hoped they lived far from his jurisdiction.

* * * * *

"Now, we can do this one of two ways. I know you've got to have some cash stashed around the house. So, you can tell us where it's at and we'll kill you fast, or you can make us search for it and we'll kill you slow—you know, skinning you to the bone bit by bit. Now, Jackie is hoping you don't tell us a thing. She really gets into the causing pain thing. But, I'd like to get out of this place, so talk!"

"Heather, you don't want to do this," Catherine blurted out, but was cut off.

"Shut up, bitch. You don't know what I want. You're not getting out of this. Now, tell me where your cash is or Jackie's gonna have some fun."

"I don't keep cash in the house. I never did. Jim used to, but I always told him it was dangerous. I do everything by credit or debit card."

Pain shot through the back of her upper left arm as the steel blade sunk to the bone. Catherine's right hand shot up to hold in the blood and saw Jackie licking the long blade.

"Oh, look, you got some on your shirt," Catherine blurted out.

By instinct, Jackie's head tilted down. Ramming forward, Catherine knocked her off balance and sent her tumbling over the arm of the couch. Running to the door, a hand clutched at her shoulder, but Catherine's flying elbow met Heather's face, stunning her. Wasting no time, Catherine flew through the door and escaped the confines of the house.

Damn, my keys are in my purse. Got to get to the barn. I can find weapons in there. Reaching the barn, she hopped inside and looked for a place to make a stand. Before climbing the ladder to the loft, she took hold of an old, rusty machete used years before to cut down some bamboo she'd thought would provide a windbreak. Up the rungs and behind a couple of bales of hay, she watched as the two attackers entered.

"You got me, old woman," Jackie's voice rang out. "Damn good job—I have to congratulate you. Been a long time since someone got the best of me. Of course, you've only delayed the inevitable, but what the hell, you know that. You're gonna die. Might as well say your last prayers."

"Jackie's right," Heather's voice rang out. "I'm gonna get you just like I got your husband years ago. Why do you think he walked out on you, anyway? He couldn't get enough of it. I hated him but knew I could get his money if he got away from you. He bled good. I got him during sex one night with a butcher knife just before he came. His face was so funny."

Her giggles echoed in Catherine's head. *So, this slut was the reason Jim left me. I'll be damned. Well, she may have got him, but she's not going to get me. No way in Hell is that going to happen!*

She listened as the two searched the bottom. Finding nothing, Catherine saw the ladder shift as one of their feet contacted the bottom rung. Silently, stepping over the hay bale, Catherine gently rolled toward it—machete in hand.

Rung after rung, the climber grew closer. As Heather's came into sight, Catherine sprang into action. Swinging the machete down with all her might, the splitting of a skull crunching broke the silence. Jackie screamed below as Heather's lifeless body thudded on the concrete floor and the machete clattered as it was thrown from the crevice it had created.

"You fucking bitch! I'm gonna make you pay, God am I gonna make you pay!"

Searching the loft, Catherine couldn't find any type of a weapon to use for protection. It was down to breaking a promise or dying.

Closing her eyes, Catherine concentrated on seeing through her mind instead of her eyes. She envisioned Jackie rushing up the rungs, reaching the top, and about to climb off the ladder. But, the ladder swayed backward, pulling far away from the loft, and rising almost to the tin roof far above. Thirty feet in the air, the ladder began to spin, slow at first and then faster. Jackie held on the best she could, knowing a drop would bring either death or paralysis.

Catherine imagined the ladder bucking as it spun—like a mechanical bull—causing Jackie to lose her hold. Flying through the air, Jackie bounced against the wall, her feet flailing, as her back slid down upon the steel tines of a pitchfork hanging on its wall hooks. Jackie struggled as they entered her back, sinking deeper with each move. It seemed as if the screams would never stop.

Opening her eyes, Catherine looked across the way to where Jackie's body hung. No more threats, no more violence upon the innocent, and no more screams—she was dead. "Damn, Bitch, I thought you enjoyed pain! All talk, weren't you?"

Her last foster mother had called it the Devil's Gift and made her promise to never call upon it. This had been the first time she had done so since the promise was made. It was necessary this time. It had saved her.

Having telekinetic powers and not being able to call upon them had been difficult. She could have pulled Jim away from the car and talked to him more, maybe even kept him from leaving. Farm work could be easier if she used her powers to move heavy items with it instead of muscles. But, she had promised.

Well, since my promise has been broken, I might as well start using my powers again. I've got two bodies to move and bury—one hanging on the wall. The gift would make getting it down much easier. Besides, no sense in bringing back the police. This mess would be too hard to explain. Maybe God will forgive me and maybe he won't. Can't worry about that right now. I gotta get down out of this loft. Let's see if I can make the ladder come back up here.

* * * * *

Gabriela lies atop the loveseat arm at my side. Her snores, though not as loud as she had told me mine were, present a distraction to my writing. I reach out and stroke her fur—not wanting to awaken and upset the demon—only wishing to quiet by comforting. Her last two tales have been impressive. I want to hear others but have no desire to face her wrath. We have reached a stage of acceptance.

Stretching, Gabriela arches her back. A yawn displays the razor-sharp incisors she knows how to use only too well. An orange glow appears from the slits of her eyes, but gradually darkens to the standard beady black.

I'm in a danger zone. She is usually not friendly upon awakening.

"You're lucky I had finished my dream," she whispers in my brain. "Otherwise, I might be tempted to slash your arm off at the shoulder."

"I thought you could use a little loving," I replied, rubbing her under the chin and around the ears. "You were snoring so loud I thought a nightmare might be taking you away."

"Good intentions will save you this time. But, in the future, I warn you to be careful. The ferocity of a bear awakened in mid-winter can be deadly. I resemble that remark."

"Well, now that you're awake, feel like telling me about your third life?"

"You've become a masochistic bastard, haven't you? A real glutton for tales of my life of misery. Gluttony is why I went back to Hell after my second life. I was judged a glutton for all the mice I'd eaten while living in the barn. It's one of the Seven Deadly Sins. Well, you caught me in a good mood. I was just dreaming about that life and remembering the good times I haa—before it went bad. Give me a few minutes to get myself together and I'll tell you about it."

Getting to her feet, Gabriela jumped down from the loveseat and took off toward the kitchen. I heard her crunching a few bites of dry food and then the unmistakable sounds of cat litter hitting the side of the litter box. She returned to the arm of the loveseat and smiled. "A girl's gotta do what a girl's gotta do. Get ready."

Peace, Love, Death?

My second wait for rebirth taught me to learn how to read a person's mind. Previously, I had understood their actions and words, but to actually travel inside of a human mind is very complicated. Weeding through your fantasies and actual thoughts, and determining which is which, is exceptionally difficult. To make it worse, the recreational drugs many experimented with in the early '70's added to the complexities.

For a second time, I was born in a dirty alley. Soon after finishing with my nursing phase, I wandered upon a young girl sleeping in a large refrigerator box. By her side was an open box of cereal, some sort of sugar coated brand. Figuring she must be done with it, I scooted into the box and started eating. I'd only taken my second mouthful when the box caved in, coming close to sending me to life Number Four. I struggled to scoot out, but the slippery wax paper inside made it impossible to get a foothold. About to pass out under the pressure, I felt my tail being pulled as the weight atop my body lightened.

"Hey, you're not a rat. You're a little kitty. Aw, you're cute. Wow, like you're all black. I bet you have magical powers."

Hands wrapped around my body, pulled me free, and lifted me away from the box of sugary delights. Immediately in front of me was the smiling face of a girl in her teens. Leaning over, she rubbed her forehead against mine, cooing at the softness of my fur, and giggling as my tail brushed her nose.

I'm glad she liked it—I didn't. In the cat world, rubbing foreheads is a sign of making one their own. We'd just met, and I accepted no such bond. Before bowing to her demands, I would need to know more about her.

Reading her thoughts, I found she meant no harm. Ignorant of the ways of felines, she was only doing what most stupid humans do—displaying their affection without caring if it's desired or not. In honesty, I've never been one to want the scent of humans rubbed all over my body, but curious as to what she'd do next, I let her get away with it.

"You're such a sweetie. I'm gonna call you Moon Magic. We'll be Moon Magic and Moonglow Meg—the double "M's", twice as good as the candy." Chuckling, she cradled me in her arms and began rubbing my tummy. God, it was amazing!

We stayed like that for over an hour—me milking Meg for all the loving absent in my previous life in the barn. Thinking back, it was one of the most enjoyable times I've ever had.

By mid-morning, Meg gathered her things from the box, stuffed them in a huge burlap bag type of purse, and we left the alley behind. After a few blocks, we came upon a huge group of people, dressed like Meg—jeans, T-shirts, and sandals. Many carried signs and banners that read

"Stop the War" and "Peace, Love, Dove" and chanted the phrase "United We Stand, Divided We Fall." Before I knew it, we were all marching down the center of the street.

There were people on the sidewalk screaming at those in the street. I was almost hit by a beer bottle thrown at Meg and watched a marcher behind us take a rock to the ear. The violence against us escalated when the police arrived. Wearing riot helmets and protective vests, they indiscriminately swung their Billy clubs at the marchers and beat many to the ground. As if that wasn't enough, my natural enemy, dogs, were released and viciously attacked all attempting to escape. I was terrified!

Meg, recognizing my plight, put me in her bag. Although hidden from sight, I knew the dogs could still smell me. Trembling at the thought of being gobbled up in one bite, I noticed a horrible, burning smell—like sulfur but worse. I heard someone holler, "Tear gas." Whatever it was, it made breathing almost impossible and burned my eyes without mercy.

Though I couldn't see or smell, I could hear Meg screaming. I was bruised as the bag banged against her hip as she fought to escape. Miles had to have been traveled before we came to a halt. Wheezing for breath, I could make out her blurred face seeking a hiding place from those still in pursuit. I felt it time to remind her of my presence and let out a few meows. I wasn't happy about my new bruises and longed to be back in the safety of the alley.

"Oh, you poor thing," lifting me out of my cloth prison. The fresh air refreshed my lungs and cleared my vision. My sense of smell returned. We were back to normal—and then she pulled the damn rubbing foreheads trick, again. "I won't let those mean pigs hurt you. I promise."

Yeah, you do that. And, get your damn face out of mine. You're all sweaty and you stink!

We ended up hiding in some bushes in a small city park. In the distance, sirens blared and a few gunshots could be heard. We were joined by a few more protesters, also hiding from the police cruisers. I kept hearing "it was supposed to be a peaceful march" by the new arrivals. Obviously, they didn't realize the Deep South was not the place to hold a protest march.

"Those bastards should all be shot. They had no reason to attack us that way. We weren't doing anything wrong. The pigs just wanted an excuse to hurt us. If these are people of God, I'm proud to worship Satan."

At the mention of the Dark One, I looked up to see if I might recognize the one speaking. He was unfamiliar to me and much older than any of the others. His hair, shorter than most, was as black as my fur. With the wrinkles showing deep on his face, I guessed it to be dyed to give him a younger look.

Listening to him talk, it wasn't hard to see many weren't impressed by his words. "The establishment isn't Satan, they are the representatives of God. This is the same God that has sent men to kill others for years so that the rich can profit. He's an evil being, one that cares not for the common man. If you protest the killing of humans, you must protest this God and turn to Satan. Only he can save you."

Most left the gathering at that time, jeering at his comments. Prior environmental conditioning with years of church attendance behind them, the man's words didn't make sense. Angry at their lack of understanding, he continued until only Meg and the lady he'd arrived with remained listening.

Being fresh to this time period, I was not aware of all that had been taking place. To me, his words made some sense, especially if one was ignorant of what Hell was really like. It was true, people protesting the killing of other humans had been attacked with a malicious intent to injure, or even kill. And, the ones attacking had been police officers, representing the law. In my past two lives, killing had been wrong, either by humans or beasts. So, why were those protesting killing being attacked? Had the world gone crazy in the time I'd been waiting to be reincarnated?

I learned the man's name to be Jacob, and the woman's Celeste. Focusing their arguments on Meg, they covered the same points repeatedly, as if brainwashing her. Although Meg listened intently, I found them hypocritical. They preached peace with Satan, but also wanted to kill all pigs. They were the same as those that attacked us—destroy all that don't agree with your opinion types. I soon grew bored and closed my ears to their orations. Weary from all that had happened, I took a nap.

When I stirred from my slumber, the daylight was almost gone. I was shocked to find Meg had accepted an invite to crash at Jacob and Celeste's place for the night. I doubted the wisdom of this decision and worried she might be in danger. Still, it was her choice. And, it had been a long time since those two mouthfuls of cereal that morning.

Keeping in the shadows, we stuck to the backstreets and alleys leading to Jacob's pad. Meeting all my expectations, his home was worse than the mountain shack of my previous owner. In fact, I wondered about the possibility of lost relatives and kidnapped babies.

Once inside, I fought to restrain a gag reflex. Hell smelled bad, but this place would make the Devil retch. Half-eaten sandwiches, rotting fruit peels, and the decomposing of rodents still in their traps all added to the sickly aroma. Not surprising in the least, the first thing Jacob did was reach for a couple of sticks of vanilla incense.

Sitting on Meg's lap, I checked out his wall adornments. Far from traditional, they looked to be a combination of flower children blacklight posters and various symbols reflecting his devotions to Satanism. Jacob needed much help in the interior decorating department, as well as in home repair and cleanliness.

For hours, Meg sat listening to him go on about the benefits of Satanism and the beauty of Hell, as if he were a constant visitor. What he was saying couldn't have been more wrong. I smiled thinking about him being a permanent occupant there in the future, being tortured again and again. I might even wave at him during one of my visits.

Engrossed in his words, Meg's interest scared me. She was so young and easily influenced by those around her. I entered her mind. She was confused, but anxious to hear more. Celeste wasn't helping matters. Sitting on the edge of a stained couch cushion, rocking back and forth, mesmerized by Jacob, her vibes helped to fortify Meg's involvement.

I'm not sure if Jacob ran out of bullshit to say, or if he got tired of talking, but he finally took a break. He walked to the stereo selected an album to play. "How about some music?"

Thanks for asking. What if I said, 'No thanks. I want to watch television. You would be screwed, wouldn't you?"

Luck would have it the music was by a super guitar player I'd seen in Hell. *Great guy, but had a habit of playing the national anthem extremely loud and distorted.* Anyway, he opened a drawer and pulled out a bag of marijuana, my old nemesis. It had been one of my minor tortures in Hell. Oh, I enjoyed the high, but munchies always followed smoking. My torture consisted of dealing with them. One could either grab some food and satisfy the cravings or keep your place in line. I cost myself at least two years of waiting before learning to bring a box lunch with me.

As a small kitten, it didn't take much to give me a contact high. Starving, I slipped away from the group while they continued to indulge. Roaming around the house, I searched for a nice fat mouse to calm my growling stomach. I figured there had to be a few living in the filth. Unfortunately, Meg noticed my absence and began to call out my newly given name. Oddly, Jacob panicked, and rushed to find me.

I had just entered a room where a horrid smell brought back early memories. It was the same smell that I'd dealt with after Amy's body had begun to decompose in my first life. The other odors had masked it initially, but now, in the same room, there was no question. But, before I could investigate further, Jacob snatched me up.

"You've no business in here, bitch," he spat out, holding the scruff of my neck none too gently. "Stay with Meg or you'll be very sorry."

So, my feelings proved correct. There was more to this ass than protesting and preaching. The bastard was a murderer.

Meg was sitting by herself when I was dropped in her lap. Once again, she did the forehead trick that drove me crazy, but it was better than being carried around by Jacob who had headed toward the kitchen. I could hear a butter knife clattering against the side of a mayonnaise jar in the kitchen, meaning Celeste was fixing sandwiches. I jumped off Meg's warm lap and headed to see what the menu would offer, doing my best to stay out of Jacob's sight.

"Here, take this to Meg," Celeste whispered. "I didn't put as much in her drink as you did last time. Maybe we'll be able to keep this one alive until we need her."

I ran back and lay against Meg's ankles as her food and drink arrived and was set upon the coffee table in front of her. As he returned to the kitchen, I climbed up her feet and did my best to leap up to the tabletop but fell short. I tried a couple of more times, desperate to be in a position to knock over her drink.

"Oh, you poor thing, you're hungry." Well, I was, but that wasn't why I kept jumping at the table, dummy. "Here's some meat for you, baby. I don't eat much meat, anyway."

Of the two options, saving her or eating, my stomach chose. My chances of knocking over her drink were much less than filling my tummy, even if it did mean eating the meat off the filthy floor. It wasn't much, but it was better than nothing.

"I know she has to be thirsty. Jacob, could you get my baby a little water?"

Somewhat begrudgingly, he agreed. I followed him, watching as he took a dirty dish from the sink and put some water in it. "Now, don't piss in the house," he said, setting it down.

Why? Are you afraid the smell of urine might make your place smell better?

Avoiding the rotten pieces of cole slaw floating on the water's surface, I drank what I could and returned to Meg. She was having a hard time keeping her eyes open, thanks to whatever Celeste had put in her drink, I was sure. Recognizing their success, Jacob and Celeste exchanged smiles as Meg's eyelids fluttered and closed one last time. It was then they went into action.

Jacob backed an old van up to the rear steps of the house. Together, they loaded Meg inside. Not wasting any time, the two added the corpse from the other room next to her. Not wanting to be left behind, I jumped inside from atop the rear steps and hid myself between the two. Meg wasn't the smartest of humans, but she had been kind to me. I had to find a way to help her.

The van was in as good a shape as Jacob's house. The engine died at stop lights, the brakes squealed whenever called upon, and the shocks no longer cushioned the ride. Bump after bump, the lights of the city were left behind. We exited the main road after an hour or so, leaving the hum of the pavement for the quiet of a dirt one. Our speed slowed substantially as ruts bounced us from side to side. Leaves and branches began scraping along the side of the van as the road became no more than a narrow path. Yep, we were well into the boondocks.

My wishes for the journey to end were soon answered. Stopping the van, Jacob left us all for a few minutes. Meg had yet to stir from her slumber—breathing shallow but regular. Whatever drug they'd used had done its job well. Celeste, staring into the darkness ahead, hummed some rock tune and mumbled the words, "This is the end" repeatedly. She stopped only after a blazing fire appeared in front of the van and Jacob flung open the van's rear doors.

"Help me get her out. Time's a wastin!"

I knew my time of discovery was soon, so I ran out the rear and leaped between Jacob's legs to the ground. Scurrying off, I hid under a thorn bush. I was almost disappointed when he gave no chase to find me. Sitting there listening to the bullfrogs talk to each other in the swamp about the crickets' noisy chirping, I pushed to come up with some sort of a plan.

The two laid Meg in front of the crackling fire and returned to the van—stirring up dust from ashes of previous fires along the way. Obviously, this wasn't a first time happening for them.

I watched as they struggled to carry the corpse over to the water's edge. Jacob, growling at Celeste and her lack of strength, grew angrier with every step. "Damn it, pick up your end. She's not that heavy. Maybe I should toss you in, too, for all you're worth."

A loud splash and the deed was done. No more evidence of the murder. There was no doubt Meg would the next to join her there.

Returning to where Meg lay, Jacob and Celeste wasted no time in first stripping off their clothes and then removing Meg's. Jacob used a long knife to make a six-inch slice at the top of Meg's thigh—smearing the blood that flowed from her wound all over his body, and then Celeste's. Satisfied at his work, Jacob stood by the fire and began chanting. Celeste placed herself next to Meg and rhythmically swayed back and forth, channeling the young girl's energy into Jacob. Soon, she joined in the chants, too.

It didn't take a genius to figure out these two had no idea as to how to perform proper Satanic Worship procedures or chants. Aside from the "Hail Satan's" and the "Our God of Darkness" phrases they filtered in, most of what they were saying was only mumbo jumbo. And, the act of human sacrifices went out of style centuries ago. Hell's big man had so much more fun tricking people into signing their souls away, that he put an end to the those taken involuntarily. Shaking my head at their stupidity, an idea hit me. I ran my little legs off to where they had tossed the corpse into the swamp water.

Hoping the two had drawn a gathering with their disposal of the body, it didn't take long for me to find what I was after. Hearing a hiss, I jumped off to my left, barely avoiding the jaws of a huge, twelve-feet-long alligator wanting another a midnight snack. Staying just outside of the range of his snapping jaws, I teased him by darting close and then pulling back. Stirring up the night with his attacks, his actions soon attracted another, even larger. Now, I had two monsters pursuing me. It was just what I wanted.

The light of the fire broke through the brush and I ran to Meg's side. Jacob and Celeste were deep in chant, eyes closed, and arms raised to the heavens above.

Celeste's eyes bulged open as two rows of jagged teeth clamped around her torso. She barely had time to scream before her ribcage was crushed. Jacob opened his eyes to see Celeste being thrashed about and torn in half.

Confident he had Satan's protection, he reached for the dagger to complete the sacrifice. Holding it high, he yelled out, "In the name of Satan, I send thee!" But, before he could bring it down, the other gator launched its attack, hitting him from behind. My elation turned to shock as he fell forward from the blow, arm flailing, and managed to sink the blade deep into Meg's chest.

I sat and watched the reptile tear off one of his legs, thrilled at the agony Jacob was enduring. Suffer you bastard, suffer! No amount of pain would compensate for his killing of Meg. Two smaller gators, attracted by the commotion, joined in and ripped smaller bites of bloodstained flesh from his arms and torso. I relished in his screams for as long as they lasted.

Watching the gators feast, I was overcome with sorrow. Meg's body had been untouched by the reptiles and lay silent. The handle of the knife stood still between her breasts, undisturbed by any hint of life existing. The poor girl never had a chance. She would be another forgotten teenager listed as "missing" until her parents either gave up hope or passed away. If the gators didn't eat her tonight, they would return to do the job. Maybe it was better than ending up like the decomposing corpse they'd tossed away without remorse.

I'd succeeded in drawing the gators to rid us of Jacob and Celeste, but my plan had been flawed. My owner was dead. We had shared only one day together, but I shed a tear in respect for kindness she had showed.

It was all I had time for. Another gator that I'd failed to notice, sent me back to Hell, waiting in line for my next life. The attack had been without warning, of course, and there had been only a second of intense pain as the jaws ripped my head from my body. Another flaw in my plan, obviously.

I hope the bastard choked on my fur. Maybe, I even gave him a hairball.

* * * * *

"So, you've dealt with a husband killer, Bigfoot creatures, and Satanic worshipers … anything else that might interest me besides the normal stuff?"

"What do you want, fake Hollywood monsters or real ones? There are all types of creatures roaming the Earth,"

she responded. "Some have mutated over the years and learned to fit into society. Others only use the human form to find prey."

"Got any good stories about them? You know, something that might make my readers happy instead of sleepy."

"You are hard to please, aren't you? Okay, here's one that I heard in Hell from one of the inmates. Strange guy—used to talk like one of those 1940's movie detectives. Listen up!

Damn Whiskers

Ever notice how a mustache always finds a way to allow one or two whiskers to get inside your mouth with every bite of food? I realize I'm talking to a select few as none of the members of the female gender with which I'm acquainted have mustaches and neither do many of my male friends. But, if you're one of us that grow facial hair, you can obviously relate. It's a pain in the ass. Every bite is followed by fingers searching to ensure it is a mustache and not one of those gnarly black monstrosities from the waiter's forearms.

I first noticed the girl as I left my Biology 221 class. Leaning back against the wall, she made herself small to allow the herd to exit. Her lean figure—with exaggerations in all the right places and silhouetted by the blinding glare of the sun exploding through the far window—emptied my mind of what I'd learned in class and filled it with ideas of how I'd love to spend my evening. A thigh-length black sweater—tight where it needed to be but loose enough to keep one guessing—presented the perfect backdrop to accent golden strands of blonde hair riding upon her shoulders. And, her face, oh, her face, was one to cause beauty queens to spit at their make-up artists for failing to make them as beautiful. High cheekbones, narrow chin, and a cute little nose set the scene for her full lips that made me yearn to say, "Come here, I can't live without you."

Yeah, I'm a male pig, I know it. But, there are times in a person's life they simply can't help themselves. Some women look at men in the same way but won't admit it. Makes them less ladylike, I've heard. I prefer one who speaks her mind. It saves a lot of time getting to the point … and the action.

What really hit me were her eyes. Strange, because I'm not normally an "eye" person. Like I said, I'm a male pig. My eyes are usually drawn to boobs and butt, and, if there are great legs attached, so much the better. Yet, this time it was different. (So, I lie a little. You already caught me drooling over her body.) Seriously, her eyes were unlike any I'd ever seen. In a good way, not like they were cross-eyed or anything. Black as a closet in a kid's bedroom at night, they gave no indication as to what secrets or stories they contained. When they met mine, the world stopped spinning and I was thrown into the depths of space en route to foreign planets and digging it. (Yeah, like there's romance in outer space.) The back of my head burned as her gaze searched deep within me, investigating my thoughts and dreams, seeking a reason to look further. I hoped she found one.

My total observation took all of three seconds. I walked fast and passed by her without a word. This girl was out of my league, big time. I'm not the worst thing to look at, but there are many who would win the World's Sexiest Man title ahead of me. Besides, I'm kind of an introvert. Girls like this expect to be saved by a superhero and carried off on a white horse to some exotic fortress of luxury and ecstasy. My efficiency apartment was anything but that.

The next day, I'm sitting in the grass in the campus wooded area called, "The Commons." Like everyone else daydreaming there, I've got an open textbook in my lap that's being totally ignored. From around the corner of the last building, Miss Heavenly Body strolls out. As before, she's impeccably dressed and draws plenty of stares from guys, like myself. We all knew we had no chance with the babe but wanted to remember everything about her for our imaginary lover sessions later.

I tilt my head down, like I'm reading, but my eyes keep rising to sneak a quick glance, without getting caught. Hoping to steal another peek, I look up and see her coming my direction. Just what I need, a woman that wants directions, hopefully to my place, but probably the library.

"I saw you coming out of class yesterday," she said in a heavy Eastern European accent. "Is there a reason you don't want to talk to me?"

Don't want to talk? Hell, I'd love to talk to you and a whole lot more. But, after being turned on by your deep, throaty voice, I'm going to sound like a stuttering child at their first circus. The pressure's on. I've got to sound smooth and witty, charming even. Yeah, like that's going to happen.

"No," I replied, drawing a blank check for any other words in the English language. This girl had me at "is."

"Well, my name is Mihaela," she offered. "Do you have a name, or shall I call you "Quiet Man?"

"I'm Adam. Good to meet you Mihaela. Ah, I love your accent. Where is it from?"

Every relationship has a starting point. Many have ending points, too, but I didn't want to think about that. I was too busy remembering what a friend of mine had said about being in a conversation with a member of the opposite sex. "You don't have to be a great talker, just a great listener. Respond to what they're saying and ask questions. They'll not only think you're interested in finding out about them but will appreciate your attention."

Somehow, I managed to keep the conversation going for about an hour, which was about twenty minutes too long for me to make a class on time. I didn't care. I was too busy wondering why any girl—this beautiful and intelligent—would want to talk to a guy like me. Maybe I reminded her of an old third grade boyfriend—one she had before she became beautiful and her body developed. I knew that couldn't be it. This girl had always been beautiful and probably needed to wear a bra as soon as she stopped wearing diapers.

Then, it hit me. It didn't matter. We were here conversing, laughing, and getting along well. Ulterior motives could lock themselves in the police files under "I Don't Give A Damn" and stay hidden forever. I simply wanted to enjoy the moment and pray it would never end. Some prayers are never answered.

She looked at her watch and said she had to get to class. My heart broke knowing my dream girl would be walking out of my world and into one filled with better looking guys. I guess that's why I was amazed when she leaned over and took my hand, saying, "We will see each other again, won't we?"

Yeah, Mr. Cool scrambled for the right answer. I remembered an old movie line and said, "Whenever you wish." I patted myself on the back knowing it would be a winner, unless she'd seen the movie—the two actors had never seen each other again in it.

Anyway, she looks deep into my eyes and, with a slight smile, replied, "Don't say that, you may get tired of me being around. See you soon."

Flabbergasted, I watched as she jumped up and ran down the sidewalk, hoping she didn't turn around and see my tongue hanging out. I was on Cloud Nine ... stunned that she hadn't cast me aside. I knew I had very little to offer. She could have any football or basketball player she wanted. Maybe even a rocket scientist. But, for some reason, she selected me, instead. "Just what I need, a girl with low standards," I said under my breath. "I hope she keeps them there."

Then it hit me. I never got a phone number or address. I'd been so in the moment that I'd forgotten about the next one. I felt like I'd picked the right lottery numbers but lost the ticket on the way to claim my prize.

For three days, I searched. Mihaela had told me she lived off campus with her father. She had been in the United States for five years and lived in five or six different cities up and down the East Coast, from Milford to Miami. They moved often because of her father's work—some kind of educational contractor. She liked Americans, but not the way they gorged themselves on fast food, cursed too often, and took too many things for granted. Thinking back, I find it strange that she shared so much, but so little. She'd obviously had a lot of practice.

I caught up on homework over the weekend and slept late both days. I caught the end of a ballgame and the beginning of the local news. One story, in particular, blew me away. My biology class professor had been found dead. The guy had been in bed and was suspected of having had a heart attack. Circumstances surrounding the event were being investigated. To me, that meant he didn't have a heart attack. Someone killed him, or he committed suicide. My guess was the former.

Monday, I went to biology class as if I didn't know anything had happened. I figured an assistant would be teaching until the university decided on a replacement. Instead, a note taped to the door stated we'd be notified when class would resume.

The bottom dropped out and I had no parachute. This was a required class for me if I wanted to graduate this year. Last thing I wanted was to have to stick around for Summer Session because the university was screwing around. My mind was all wrapped up trying to figure out my next move when I heard a familiar voice say, "Hello, Stranger."

"Well, hello to you," I replied. At least one good thing was going to happen to me on this lousy afternoon. "I thought you'd been kidnapped by aliens or something.

Mihaela smiled. "I figured I'd find you here. Did you have a good weekend?"

"It would have been better if I could have spent it with you." *Whoa, where did that come from?* "I mean ..."

She stopped me with an index finger to my lips and a light kiss to the cheek. "Don't worry, I had to finish some things up. Now, we can spend the time together I promised."

The lady didn't lie. That night, with one candle illuminating the room, we made love in my cheap efficiency apartment. For me it was great. Mihaela seemed to enjoy herself as well. She was a beast in bed, filled with more energy than a fake bunny with new batteries.

She pushed me until I had no more to give and then made me take out a loan for more. I finally had to surrender and say, "No mas." I was used to being the horny one. This girl made me look like a wimp.

She'd drained me. Being the typical male, I passed out. I woke once during the night to go to the bathroom. The bed was empty beside me. Then, I spied her on the other side of the room watching some late-night horror movie. She was wearing only my unbuttoned flannel shirt—nothing else. After the bathroom, she helped me take the shirt off.

I didn't go to classes the next day, or the next. Mihaela kept me busy. I was her slave, there only to serve her need for sex. For a young man of nineteen, she was a dream come true. Her body took me on a world cruise and showed me all the sites. I enjoyed being a tourist.

I stayed exhausted. Even after sleep, my body couldn't cope with the amount of activity Mihaela demanded. I tried to ease my aches in a full tub of hot water. I was doing okay until she joined me there. The water didn't get cold fast enough.

By the end of the third day, I didn't care if I ever had sex again. I needed food and rest. This "No Stop Marathon" was becoming more of a task than a pleasure. My sexual appetite was full but my stomach empty. Plus, I was missing class after class—not a way to achieve passing grades.

The bathroom provided me with my only escape. By the end of the third day, I stood at the sink and saw myself in the mirror. I'd become a skeleton of myself. My transformation exceeded the realm of reality. Besides losing over twenty pounds, my hair was thinning … turning gray, and my face had wrinkles. I looked like an old man! One didn't have to be a genius to know there was more than sex involved here.

I'd been in a daze most of those three days. Mihaela's eyes had been hypnotic—big, black optic drills boring deep and removing my sense of will. She assumed complete control—taking me down a road of deadly pleasure as a kidnapped participant.

I knew it had to change and bolted to the kitchen. Opening the refrigerator, I grabbed an old package of hamburger, tore away the wrapper, and stuffed my mouth full.

Ignoring Mihaela's efforts to draw my attention, I attacked a package of lunch meat next. Strength was returning to my body. Mihaela's hands tugged at my shoulders, trying to spin me around. I cast her off and dug into a week-old pizza.

The more I ate, the stronger I got. The protein was being digested and racing to all parts of my emaciated self. I knew it wouldn't be long before I was back to normal strength.

"I've got to give you credit," Mihaela conceded, "You're mentally stronger than any nerdy loser I ever met. And, that includes that fat slob biology professor. Look at me, damn it!"

I felt the power of her command but ignored it. Continuing to stare into my empty fridge, I asked, "You're a succubus, aren't you?" I had no doubt of the fact, but I wanted to see if she'd admit it.

"So, you've guessed my secret," Mihaela replied, sounding aggravated. "Yes, I'm a succubus. If you'd look at me, you could see how much my body has improved since we started together. And, now that you're almost back in shape, it could get even better. Won't you peek?"

"Only if you poke out your hypnotizing eyes." I was offended by her feeble effort. "The professor … you were with him last weekend? So, it wasn't a heart attack."

"The bastard had it coming. He had been to a reception for my father and made some lewd passes. I told my father about his remarks and he told me to do what I do best. So, I did. You were such a change—lean, kind of like two percent milk. Tasty, but little fat."

"I suppose you're going to try to kill me to keep me quiet. How do you propose to do it? You already failed once."

"Actually, I'm going to keep you around," she growled out, like a Siamese cat in heat. I know I can always come back and finish the job later. You'll want me again. All men want me. You're all the same."

I heard her getting dressed and shut the front door. I listened to see if she'd really gone or was playing games—hoping I'd turn around and she could catch me with those eyes. After a few minutes I aimed my eyes at feet level and shot out a few glances. Mihaela had either left or was standing on the ceiling—my guess wasn't the ceiling.

I sat naked on a kitchen chair, reminiscing about her beauty and demeanor. I could've stayed with her forever under normal circumstances. But, the bitch had played me. I was nothing but food on a menu, and she could make any selection she wanted. The more I thought about it the angrier I got. She'd taken without mercy and sneered at me in the end. Completely unacceptable.

I slid on a pair of jeans and a t-shirt and hurried out the door. I ran out of the apartment complex parking lot, and after a couple of blocks, saw her walking toward campus.

Propelling forward on the balls of my bare feet, noise and vibration stayed at a minimum. I had to be careful. Mihaela wasn't the normal female. She had some of my life's energy still in her. No telling what she could do.

Less than half a block away from her, I ducked behind a Sycamore tree and shed my clothes. Once I had changed, it was easy to catch up and lurk in the bushes beside the sidewalk. As I had guessed, she was taking the shortcut through the park. That would make things easy.

I attacked her in the darkness between streetlights. My weight, landing atop Mihaela's shoulders, shoved her face into the fresh mowed grass. I slammed my fangs deep into the nape of her neck. Reaching around to her face, my claws ripped her hypnotic eyes from their sockets. She managed to let out a partial scream before my claws tore out her throat.

Still ravenous from her three days of sucking my energy levels dry, I shredded Mihaela's flesh, consuming most of her vital organs, until my stomach could hold no more. Before returning to my human form, I had one last use for my claws. Cutting out Mahaela's uterus may have seemed morbid and unnecessary to those finding and investigating her remains, but it made perfect sense to me.

For the next few days, local news broadcasts were filled with details about a savage attack and the mangled body discovered. Fear ruled the city and locked doors were repeatedly checked as many attempted to ensure their safety from an unknown and violent beast. Owners of larger dog breeds were questioned, public and private keepers of exotic animals investigated, and mental institutions put on alert for missing patients, but no avenue provided answers.

Besides me, only my mother knows what really happened that night. She was the only person I could trust to tell. After all, she had to know what I wanted her to do with Mihaela's uterus.

Mother's a scientist who used to perform research experiments at the university in the Biology Department. I was majoring in the subject to follow in her footsteps. She believed she could incubate a fertilized egg, nurture it outside the womb, and create a living being. Unfortunately, grant money ran out and university politics shut down her work.

I never used protection with Mihaela—she never gave me a chance. My kind has always been extremely fertile, as are those wearing the "Succubus" title. Figuring an egg had been fertilized, I did what I did.

I've always respected my mother and her work. And, she's a good mother, too. I've always loved her. And, now, so does my son!

We were talking about my childhood. the other night. She laughed about how difficult it had been to keep the whiskers out of my mouth when I'd been eating--before I'd learned how to control my changing. At the time of our conversation, I was pulling one of my son's whiskers out from inside his mouth, just as she had done to mine two decades before.

It's a common problem for werewolves.

*****

"I do have to admit, I like a werewolf story. But, don't they need a full moon to change?"

"Did I say there wasn't a full moon that night?"

Thinking back, she was right. She hadn't mentioned it one way or the other. "So, do you need a break or are you ready to tell me another one?"

"If you're ready, I'm ready," she hissed. "You want another monster tale or something else. You know, maybe the story about a boy and his cow and this giant Kudzu plant in his backyard."

"You mean the one where the cat is sleeping and the cow steps on her crushing her spine?"

"No, that's another one I'll save for later. God, millions of writers alive today and I end up with this smartass."

Help Me

I should have my head examined for thinking I could make this trip in a sports car. Dean McKenna shook his head as the car scraped bottom. *Please don't let me get stuck, not out here. It's too late to think about finding a phone to call a tow truck.*

His poor car was packed. From the passenger seat and floor to the trunk, he had stuffed it with all he would need for his short stay in the woods. Dean's frustration was aggravated by the thought of the pick-up truck he'd reserved at the rental office, still sitting there. Thanks to a work emergency, he had arrived late to find the office closed. Refusing to wait until they opened in the morning, he decided to make do with his two-seater. Deep rutted dirt and gravel roads filled with crater sized potholes were making him regret his decision.

A few years before, Dean had purchased a plot of land and a small cabin. Set deep in the forest, civilization was left behind—along with all the stress and pressure he dealt with daily. The three-hour drive there was a pain in the ass, as was the gratuitous cleaning that started each of his semiannual visits. He had a new roof put on to keep out the rains and snows, and new heavy doors to keep out trespassers and hopefully, bears. His fortress of solitude was an expensive venture.

For all the cabin's trouble, it was a relaxing place. The quiet of the forest allowed him to meditate and the fresh air cleaned the city smog from his lungs. He needed it to refresh his brain—to clear out the frustrating office politics and constant fear of false allegations from those looking to make a quick buck from the company's fear of challenging accusations.

Dean usually made the journey earlier in the day so that he could enjoy the sights along the way. The transition from city to country brought about a relief in him—one that said, "Goodbye, I'm officially out of here. You idiots enjoy the chaos while I'm gone!"

Tonight was the first time he had traveled these dirt roads through the dense woods in the darkness. He felt a sort of uneasiness, a feeling of being watched from the shadows behind the trees that lined his way. Shaking off a shiver, he smiled to himself, "Get it together—it's only your imagination, old man."

Another scrape of the car's undercarriage against hidden rock in the weeds brought his attention back to the road. *You should have got the pick-up last night, you dumbass. Pay a hundred grand for a sports car and ruin it driving to a cabin. And, what if it rains? I'll be stuck here until the roads dry out. Got any other smart moves planned?*

Finally, the red mailbox that marked his driveway showed up in the headlights. Turning in, the car bounced up the overgrown path and stopped thirty feet from the cabin. Sitting back,

Dean cut off the engine and took a deep breath. In the beams illuminating the front of the cabin, he noticed something wrong—the front door of the cabin was wide open.

What the hell, did someone break in? I don't need this, not now, not tonight. If all my stuff is gone I'm screwed. No way I can take this car back and forth trying to restock everything. Hope no bears or snakes have made it their home.

Grabbing his .45 automatic out of the glove compartment, Dean stepped out of the car and listened for any signs of movement. Nothing. Deciding a warning might save him a close encounter, he shouted out, "If there's anyone inside, let me know now or you will be shot on sight!"

His voice sounded as if reverb had been added as it echoed through the woods. There seemed to be only silence—no sign of movement in or outside the cabin. Even the crickets had stopped singing for the moment. "I'm not kidding. Come out of there."

Nothing. He looked at the pistol in his hand, knowing the last thing he wanted to do was use it on someone or something. Yet, he didn't have a lot of options. There was no way he was going to drive fifteen miles back down that hellish road to get to a store and call the police. What could he tell them, that the door was open? The store would be closed anyway. Besides, what could be in there that his pistol couldn't handle?

Reaching into the door pocket, Dean grabbed his tactical flashlight and switched it on high. Along with his headlights, the front of the cabin was completely lit up. Flashlight in one hand and gun in the other, he advanced up the front steps to the open door. "One last time, I'm armed and will shoot to kill. If anyone's in there let me know now and I'll let you go free."

Using Hollywood movie police tactics, Dean entered, swinging the pistol and light from side to side. Having checked out the cabin to find it empty, he lit up the three oil lanterns and set them around the inside. Shadows eliminated, he could relax a bit while he took inventory.

The cabin was as it had been left. Dusty cans of soup and vegetables lined the two by four shelves he'd nailed up in the corner. Below them, a pot, skillet, and a couple of pans hung from their nails. Even the metal tub he used for washing stood undisturbed on the wooden table in the center of the room. As far as he could tell, nothing had been stolen.

The floor showed no evidence of any footprints or dirt having been tracked inside. He did see quite a few rodent droppings in the corners—and one live mouse scurried across the wooden bed frame leaning against the wall. *Hey, little fellow, it wasn't you that broke into my place, was it?*

Relieved that nothing inside the cabin was amiss, Dean unloaded the car. Settling in, he lit a fire in the pot-bellied stove for warmth and took a seat at the table. *Why would someone break-in and not steal anything? What had they hoped to find—a treasure of some sort?*

Dean had never associated with any of the locals besides the elderly clerks at the store way down the road. Even then, it had been only small talk. He always paid in cash for the supplies he bought there but was careful to never show bills larger than a twenty. He had no need to draw attention by flashing around a lot of cash. The break-in simply didn't make sense.

Having used the last of the wood on the fire, Dean headed out to see if what he had cut last visit was still there. Hesitating at the door, he aimed the flashlight where the steel hasp and padlock had been. The wood was splintered, as if the two had been ripped out of the frame. Someone strong must have been desperate to get in. But why?

Reaching the woodpile, the light shining from the lanterns inside showed it still piled high. After a couple of trips with split logs, he grunted as he climbed back on the porch. *Father Time and sitting on his butt in the office is having an effect on me. Time to get back to the gym.* Dean swayed with the weight, almost losing his balance, and falling back. Steadying himself, he took a couple of steps toward the front door. Ahead of him, leaves were rustling.

Damn, I left my pistol on the table! Rushing inside, Dean dropped the wood by the stove and grabbed his weapon. Holding the cold steel in his hand gave him renewed bravery.

Grabbing his flashlight, Dean inched his way out of the door, shining the light in the direction he had heard movement. Brightness lit up the forest for over fifty yards, but only his old outhouse stood alone in the weeds. Taking his time approaching it, the sound of dried leaves being stirred about broke the silence. Throwing open the door, he jumped back as a raccoon hissed an angry warning and ran out.

"You little bastard," a smile crossing his face as the tension eased. "You've got the whole woods to crap in. Stay out of my outhouse." Glancing inside, Dean saw an open roll of tissue being used to soften a bed of leaves on the floor. Shaking his head, he returned to the cabin.

Dean leaned against the heavy door and slid the thick wooden bar into its metal brackets on each side. *That should keep visitors out for tonight.* He had purchased the open bar lock after being awakened by the sounds of a curious bear one morning. Not wanting to have a houseguest, he'd shopped around and installed the lock on his next visit. It wasn't a guarantee against a bear getting in, but strong enough to provide plenty of warning if one tried.

Though late, Dean spent the next hour cleaning up. A can of soup warmed atop the stove supplied his evening meal. Exhausted, he set up the bed frame, blew up the air mattress, and settled down for the evening. Several times in the night, Dean's sleep was bothered by strange noises. Too tired to care, he quickly went back to sleep. *As long as they're out there and I'm in here, I don't care what's roaming around.*

Dean awoke with the sun blinding him. Climbing out of his sleeping bag, he gazed out the window. Before him was the reason he bought the place—pure beauty. This was the wilderness—towering trees and thick brush, all heavy with dew, sparkling with the sun's rays shining down from the heavens. It was amazing.

Standing still and barely breathing, Dean admired his view. He was lucky to be here at this moment surrounded by nature's beauty instead of six lanes of metal monsters all vying for positions as they raced upon cement highways, seeing who could cut off the other person first. The drive the night before, the suspense of the open door and ripped off lock, and even the noises in the night had all been worth it -- a small price to pay for paradise.

A chill swept through him. *Of course, the fire burned itself out overnight. Time to get it going again.*

Using a bottle of water to prime the pump, he filled up an old coffee pot and set it atop the stove. Waiting for the coffee to brew, he relaxed a few minutes. It wasn't long before Dean was swigging down fresh brewed coffee and attacking a package of cinnamon rolls. Stuffed, he sat back with a smoke and gave the inside a quick inspection. In the light of day, it was obvious that his efforts the previous night had only scratched the surface. There was still much that needed to be done. *Too many spider webs in the rafters. I need to get up there and clean them out before I get bit. Wait a minute … what's that?*

High above the door, lightly scratched into a rafter, were the words, "Help Me."

A shiver ran through Dean's body, shaking the ash off the end of his cigarette and onto the table. Pulling his chair under the rafter, he stepped up and stretched to get a better look. The letters had been scratched into the board multiple times. Whoever had done the deed hadn't used a knife, rather something much duller. The thickness of each line was seemingly etched with a dull pencil, yet, there were no telltale lead markings. Could something have clawed the letters into the rafters? If so, what kind of creature could write these dire words?

A sharp rapping caught him off guard and nearly sent him tumbling. *Who in the world could that be? I've never had a visitor here.*

Hopping down, he started to the door, but stopped and holstered his pistol in his jean pocket. There were too many weird things taking place and being prepared for the next would be a good idea. Again, the rapping sounded.

"Okay, okay," he shouted, lifting the bar from the brackets at the door. "Have some patience."

Standing there was an old woman. Dirty, toothless, and wrinkled, the decades of struggling to survive were evident. Her eyes, beady black and full of fire, burnt deep into Dean's soul, seeking to char any resistance before it had a chance to prepare for battle. The rags, she had draped loosely over her frail body, would have been tossed out by most and replaced years before. Yet, on her, they seemed fitting.

"You got no business here," a cracking voice screeched so powerfully it silenced the birds and insects. "This here is private land, has been for years. Don't need no one tryin' to change it."

Dean, somewhat taken back by the verbal assault, did his best to respond as politely as possible. "Ma'am, I bought this property five years ago. I'm sorry we haven't met before. My name is Dean, Dean McKenna. Who might you be?"

"I be who I am … and that's none of your business," the old woman shot back. "Iffin' you know what's good for you, you'll get out. Don't want to end up like that last city fellow, do you? He found out he didn't belong here. You'd be smart to do the same."

"Ma'am, I only come up here a few weeks a year. I don't kill any animals, and I don't plan on changing a thing. I only want a few weeks to get out of the city and find some peace and quiet in the deep woods. Now, since you don't seem to want to be friends, I suggest you leave. You're on private property."

Dean had to give it to the old woman, she was not afraid to let her thoughts be known. He wondered if she had been involved in the break-in. She didn't have the strength to pull off the hasp and lock, but she might have known someone who could. There was something about her that wasn't normal … almost evil in nature.

"I'm tellin' you, get out of here. Others thought me the fool and now they wished they'd listened. Ain't safe here. Leave while you're able." Turning away, she inched off the porch and down the steps. Walking by his sports car, she spit tobacco juice on the hood and cackled the rest of the way to the dirt road.

The nerve of that bitch! Hurrying to pump some water into his soup pan at the sink, he grabbed a roll of paper towels and rushed to the car. *I can't believe her nerve, spitting on a hundred-thousand-dollar car.*

Having washed the hood clean, Dean returned to the cabin and poured himself another cup of coffee. Staring at the rafter, he sat perplexed over its message, as well as the one from the old woman.

Where does she come off threatening me? I tried to be nice, but she would have none of it. And, why does this place matter to her, anyway? Besides, what can she do to me? One thing for sure, I can't leave the door open when I do my nature walks. I've got to find that hasp and padlock and put them back up.

After a few minutes of searching, the glint of metal in the weeds off the porch's side provided the hasp. Both sides—still held together with the padlock—had been bent into a "V" from the strength of the force that had removed it. The only screw remaining in the hasp was also bent into a ninety-degree angle. With no scratches on the metal, confirmation of two things took place. One was that no tool had been used. The second eliminated any chance of the culprit being the old woman.

He attached the hasp with some extra screws and began cleaning the spider webs from the rafters inside. Before long, the place wasn't spotless, but was livable for the week ahead. Dean hoped it would at least it reduce his chance of running into a surprise visit of two-legged or eight-legged creatures.

Time to stop with this stuff and clear my head. I've got to get out of here and do what I came to do. Can't keep Mother Nature waiting.

Stuffing some canned meat, crackers, and bottled water into his backpack, he holstered his pistol and headed out the door. After padlocking the door, he grabbed an old walking stick and took to an old path he had traveled several times.

Entering the woods, the endless beauty of his surroundings demanded his full attention. Nature had done her job well. Walking among the majestic trees that seemed to stretch up into the clouds, the sights of the forest became abundant. Stopping to watch gray squirrels running along the branches and chattering as they played their meaningless games, Dean couldn't hold back his laughter. His eyes feasted on the multi-colored wildflowers that added contrast to the various shades of green leaves and played host to an array of insects. Birds burst out from bushes and soared to the branches above, providing him with a plethora of sounds and colors.

Cresting a hill, Dean stopped, taking in the picturesque scene ahead. Truly, it was one of the most heavenly sights he'd ever set his eyes upon. A lush, green meadow, several acres wide, rippled in the wind as various wildflowers danced in their own magical rhythm. A sparkling, freshwater brook, its clear waters rushing through the large blocks of stone along its banks, sparkled in the rays of the noonday sun. A small herd of deer, maybe eight or nine, roamed the far side of the meadow by the forest's edge.

The one time I don't bring my camera and I run across this. I'm just gonna soak it in and then head down to that stream. I bet it's ice cold. That would sure help my aching feet.

Sitting on a huge rock, Dean shed his boots and immersed his feet in the rushing water—yanking them back out with a yelp. *Damn, water's cold as ice! I wasn't prepared for that at all. Let's do this a little slower.*

Easing them back in, his days of playing football and the ice baths in the whirlpool after practice came to mind. They were torture, but his body always felt better afterward. Hoping for the same results, he fought to keep them submerged. Leaning back, he tried to soak up some sun and snacked on a few crackers. Summer was a couple of months away and the wind had a dampness to it. *Could be rain. Not the weather I wanted.*

The mountain water was too cold. With his feet almost numb, he pulled them out and let the sun dry them. A wave of drowsiness hit him—time for a nap. If the rains came later, this might be his only chance to get a short sleep out in the open. Settling back in the tall weeds, he drifted off.

He awoke hours later, to the echoing of chants in the night. He had overslept. The trip back to the cabin was going to be difficult in the dark. The voice in the distance was that of a female--one that sounded familiar.

Stretching his head above the weeds, Dean spotted a fire at the end of the meadow. Circling the flames was the old woman, who had confronted him earlier. She seemed to be in a trance, chanting unfamiliar words with her arms raised to the sky.

Dean reached for where he had set his boots, but they were missing. So was his backpack. Doing his best to stay out of sight, he searched all the way to the brook. *Nothing! Could that old woman have taken them? Naw, she wouldn't dare. Wait a minute, my hat's gone, too.*

In the weeds to his right, a loud growling broke the rhythm of the old woman's voice. Weaponless, Dean jerked his head in the direction from where it had come, trying to make out some form in the moonlight. There was some movement back along the tree line, but it was too vague to distinguish. He needed his backpack and gun.

Okay, this isn't good. No shoes, no weapon, and an animal of some type to deal with. God, I don't want to, but I need confront that old woman and get my stuff back. I don't have many options right now.

His stocking feet provided little protection from the briers. Dean tried to silence his 'ouches', but a few slid out before he could stop them. Less than twenty feet separated the two. Five or six more good steps and he'd be right behind her. His eyes searched for any sign of his things but found nothing.

"So, you awaken," she screeched out, turning to face him. "I was growing tired of waiting for you."

"Where are my things? You have them somewhere. Where?"

"You have no need for them any longer," she cackled through a toothless grin. "I warned you—leave—but you stayed. And, you not only stayed, you trespassed upon my land. You are stupid like the others. They learned this is not the place for your kind. But, if you want to stay, then you will stay--my way."

"Look, you're not making any sense. Just give me my things and I'll be gone."

"They are gone, gone to the fire. The spell has been cast. You have no need for things. Soon, you will be as the others in the forest--those who have their stories told to children but bring fear to the adults who dare to say their name."

"Look, enough is enough," he raised his voice as he advanced toward the woman. She threw back her head and laughed at him. Dean reached out, not knowing what he would do once he had her in his grip.

Stepping away, the old woman tripped backward over a log. Into the fire she fell, her laughter echoing from the flames engulfing her rags. "You will see. You will be like all the others."

Damn it, I didn't want this to happen. All you had to do was to give me my things. Why'd you do it? Why?

Stumbling up the hill, he felt shock and guilt making each step heavier. A chorus of howls filled the night from the meadow he was leaving behind. It was as if a mourning was taking place by wild beasts.

He recognized nothing as he entered the forest. Each step grew more difficult. His muscles stiffened, and darting pains shot up from his feet. Pushing forward, the noise of rustling leaves surrounded him. Whatever stalked him made no attempt to quiet their presence. *I've got to get to the cabin. It's my only chance. Maybe the lock bar will keep them out.*

Every move thrust more pain through his body. His clothes tightened and hindered his breathing until the seams burst, leaving the remains behind. Footsteps became thuds upon the forest floor and clattered upon pieces of rock. His head, catching in the low-lying limbs, jerked back nearly snapping his neck.

Arriving at the cabin, Dean yanked away the hasp and slammed open the door that had shrunk since he'd last passed through. Ducking, he managed to enter, amazed that he no longer needed a lantern to see. He scanned the inside, shocked that it no longer offered anything that interested him.

His fear departed as others entered behind him. Turning to face them, he saw a group, none less than eight feet tall--each with clawed paws for hands, the head of a bear, and the antlers of an elk rising from the top of their skull. Their barks and growls were now understandable.

"Welcome to our brotherhood," the closest one spoke. "Welcome to the world of Wendigo. You angered the witch. This is your curse as it is ours. We are eternally damned to roam the wilderness. Welcome to your new home."

Dean's hope of escape faded. This was what she had spoken of, it was her revenge—his penalty for ignoring her warning. Glancing up, he took two steps forward and raised his hand to the rafter, now within easy reach. He traced the letters of the words "Help Me" with his claw. The size of the grooves was a perfect match. It was all clear to him, now, but too late to matter.

** * * *

"So, are you going to church this morning?" Blurry eyed from writing all night, I wasn't in the mood for the typical Gabriela sarcasm. "After all, you do proclaim yourself to be a Christian."

"I need to finish this chapter. I think God will excuse me for missing services this week."

"What's God going to do, write a note to your preacher to keep you from being sent to detention?"

"No, God's not going to write me a note," I replied, attempting to mimic her sarcastic tone. "I'm an adult. I can make choices. I'll just be held accountable later."

"Yeah, Saint Peter gets on his computer, checks out if you've been naughty or nice, and before you know it, a corporate decision has been made—forever—no appeal."

"There are many that don't even believe in God anymore. What if God doesn't exist?"

"Yeah, the same folks that don't believe in God believe in vampires, demons, and werewolves, and are spending their Sunday nights watching zombies stroll across their television screens," she spouted out. "Humans believe in what they choose to believe and cast off the rest. Let me tell you, God's pissed off. Church attendance is down and everyone's killing everyone. There's gonna be an overpopulation in Hell, soon."

"Gabriela, is this leading up to another story?"

"Get ready to type …"

Heaven or Hell ... Your Choice

In Christianity, God is the good guy and the Devil is the bad. Like any book, the Bible needs a hero and a villain, so those two play the roles. And, like most stories, the bad guy is usually is seeking vengeance for something the good guy did to him. In this case, the Devil was an angel that pissed God off and was sent to Hell as punishment.

Now, God is the antithesis of a good guy. What hero messes around with another man's wife and impregnates her, and then sends her back to her husband? Not only that, but the husband must find a place to have the kid and raise him. Wouldn't it make sense for God to at least give them a house, or child support?

Then, the Almighty lets his kid be crucified. Why? Not because of anything the kid did, but because of God's prediction of the sins people would do in the future. I guess God forgot about having the Devil around to torture folks for that exact purpose. I can see the Devil watching and thinking, *Hey, remember me? Remember what I'm here for? You can let the kid live. Oops, guess not.*

But, somehow, God's made into a hero and is worshiped by all Christians. Sounds like an Alfred Hitchcock movie, doesn't it? But, enough on that. My take on this whole thing is probably why I keep ending up back in Hell.

One of my previous owners, the illustrious Frederick P. Tyler, prided himself on being a religious man. He was raised in a Christian home and never forgot the values of that upbringing. He was one of the few in business to incorporate his religious belief system into his daily tasks, instead of using the common methods of backstabbing and office butt kissing.

Frederick prospered during the early days of computer companies. In fact, he had even been named Managing Director of a small corporation. He prospered, went in debt on an extravagant home and expensive cars, and tithed more than generously to his church. Things couldn't have been better.

At least, that was his life before the company was bought out by a huge competitor. Of course, Frederick lost his job and was sent packing. Bill collectors did their jobs well, and soon he had lost his home, cars, and pride. We were out on the street. You know, the rags to riches story in reverse.

Having no other choice, Frederick approached the preacher and asked for the church's help. A special collection was held to help him. At the end, a check for $13.82 was presented him. Faith in God and his fellow church members didn't dwindle, it vanished completely.

One of the members of the congregation let us live in an old shed he had beside his home. It wasn't much, but it did have a wood burning stove to keep us warm. I had mice to eat, but my owner had to beg for his food. I tried offering him a mouse or two I'd caught, but he didn't seem interested.

Frustration of his plight grew. I watched him, a particular cold Sunday morning, cry out in desperation, "Devil, hear my words. Oh, Satan you bastard, if you'll make me wealthy again you can have my soul. I want vengeance on those who have snubbed their noses during my time of need. Hear me, Devil, I'm yours if you'll appease my yearning for revenge!"

I thought the flue had stuck on the stove pipe. Smoke filled the room and the familiar smell of sulfur hit my nostrils. The sounds of maniacal laughter and tortured screams—needing some sincere volume adjusting—accompanied the entrance of an old friend, the honorable Judge Clifford Richford.

Seeing me, a smile crossed the judge's face and his warm hand lay upon my back as he had done several times in the past. I always liked this guy, even if he had sentenced hundreds of innocent people to be hanged back in the 1800's. He had charisma!

"Mr. Tyler, I presume," he announced, returning his attention to my owner. "My master sends his regrets that he is unable to attend your internment but guarantees he will be available later to welcome you. I am his servant, Judge Clifford Richford, and well acquainted with the process to ensure all terms of the agreement will meet with your satisfaction. I understand that revenge upon a specific congregation is your request. Is that correct?"

My owner's mouth hung open for almost a minute after the judge had spoken. The pressure brought about by this silence was an old trick perfected by the judge and used by politicians and salespersons for over a century. Ask a question and allow silence to pressure an answer. The first person to speak is the loser. The judge was the master, planting a smile on his face and standing quiet.

Finally, my owner closed his mouth and spoke, "Yes, I want revenge on the hypocrites of the church congregation that preach brotherhood and goodwill but refuse me both."

"Excellent," whispered the judge. "We have come up with a wonderful plan. If to your liking, would you execute it without remorse?"

"I'm listening. Tell me about it."

Planting himself down upon one of the larger fire logs, the judge outlined the entire scheme. Asking closed ended questions in a manner that only allowed "Yes" as a response, he quickly closed the deal.

I watched as the judge pricked Frederick's index finger and acquired his blood signature upon the contract. I could have warned my owner that he needed to read the whole contract before signing, but the judge had already read my thoughts and recommended that I reconsider. Knowing I'd probably be back in Hell awaiting my next life, I decided my silence would be the best thing.

"Yes, yes, that's truly excellent," the judge commented as he stuck the contract inside his coat pocket. "Now, go to sleep tonight. When you awaken tomorrow, your life will be forever changed. I will be looking forward to seeing you in the future. Until then, enjoy your new life!"

And, with that, the judge walked over, gave me a final pet, and disappeared.

My owner did as he'd been told. A log on the fire, lights turned out, and off to bed he went. Sleep carried him away within seconds. I lay by the stove, listening to the wood crackle in the flames, questioning what it would take to have a normal master. Things always started good, but never ended that way.

A rapping at the door woke Frederick and myself the next morning, Loud and merciless, it continued until my owner arose and answered it.

"Frederick, sorry to wake you but I have an opportunity I hope you'll be interested in taking," rattled out the preacher of my owner's church. "My beloved secretary passed away late last night, and I am in dire need of a person that has accounting and communication skills. It doesn't pay much, but it would get you out of this shed and into a small home owned by the church. Your rent would be free, and you'd have money to eat and clothe yourself. I'd love to have you in the position. Please, tell me "Yes" so I can tell the deacons the position has been filled."

Affirming he'd take the job, he was informed the church would put him up in a hotel for a week while the previous secretary's personal items were gathered and removed by her family. He'd also get a month's salary as a sign on benefit to help him get situated. It took us all of fifteen minutes to gather up our things and get to the hotel. They didn't like having me there but finally agreed at the insistence of my owner and the preacher.

For me, it was a long week. My owner spent his days working at the church and I slept most of the time. Being a fairly clean place to stay, it was free of mice, which meant canned food for me every night. It's not bad stuff, but the fun of the chase, the crunching of bones, and the taste of fresh blood was missing. Besides, regardless of what the label says, it all tastes like chicken.

At the end of the week, we moved into the previous secretary's house. As luck would have it, she must have been a cat lover. Conveniently, there was a cat entrance by the backyard door. I could come and go as I pleased, catch a mouse or bird when I wanted, and lounge in the sun during the day. I must say, it was a nice change from the old shed.

Frederick attended every Sunday church service and Wednesday night prayer meetings. He'd come to the house afterward, laughing about those that had denied him and how they once again accepted his attendance. I learned his contract with the Devil gave him untold knowledge of the Bible and that he could quote any passage without error.

Amazed at this ability, the preacher asked him to assist with the writing of Sunday sermons. Before long, Frederick was writing them on his own. Word of his talent spread. In times of the preacher's absence, Frederick was asked to perform the services for the congregation. When cancer caused the premature death of the preacher, Frederick was unanimously chosen as the church's new minister—an honor as he was void of any formal teachings.

All was going according to plan.

We moved into preacher's residence. It was huge. It took forever to cover my daily curiosity walk through the house. Frederick, having been secretary, convinced the elders to allow him to keep that position as well as minister, and retain the salaries of both. The church purchased him a new car to visit the bedridden and provided a clothing allowance to look presentable when welcoming new attendees.

As the congregation multiplied, he began to receive a large percentage of the offerings. They went in deep debt for a larger building and filled it with all the modern lecture devices to make his sermons more entertaining. As Frederick's bank account grew, he had no qualms of taking the church further and further into debt.

Late getting home one evening, he grabbed me up and swung me around while proclaiming, "I did it. Old Mrs. Kendall will be the first to fall.

Her husband refused to give me a job or give me a penny when I was down. He'd be turning over in his grave if he knew I just had his wife sign over her estate to the church when she dies. Little does she know that's going to happen soon. I'll see to it."

Two weeks later, while making his rounds, Frederick returned to the Widow Kendall's house. With no answer at the front door, he went around to the back and found the door smashed open. Calling the police, they entered and found her naked body rotting away in the bathtub. Hiding his smile with a white handkerchief, Frederick officiated at the funeral.

Accidents began happening to the older members of the congregation. A deacon was found run over by his tractor, another fell off a ladder in his store and crashed into a glass display case—his carotid artery severed on the jagged edges. One member was crushed as a stack of lumber fell upon him at the sawmill. All accidents, but suspicious in nature.

Children of the original members found their lives in jeopardy as well. Two were found drowned in a river they'd never swam in before. Another was trampled by a spooked horse while practicing in a field behind the church. And a young boy died of multiple snake bites while fishing. He'd been found with a can of baby copperheads, one attached to the hook of his cane pole. He must have thought they were worms. (Where do you think the urban legend started, anyway?)

Only the children of Jeremy Fulk were spared. Jeremy was a poor man that had gone without lunch for a week by contributing his last ten dollars to Frederick's special offering.

Fifteen years passed quickly. I had never lived so long in one life, but I was getting old and knew my life was coming to an end. I'd grown too slow to catch mince, canned food had lost its attraction, and all I did was sleep in the sun.

At the end of a particularly warm December day, I woke to the smell of smoke and sulfur. Memories of a good friend brought a smile to my face. Opening my eyes, I spied Judge Richford sitting on the other end of the couch. Reaching over, he began rubbing the underside of my neck. My purrs were automatic.

"So, Gabriela, you've had a pretty good life, haven't you?"

"Not too shoddy this time. It was a little rough at the start, but things got better after Frederick signed up with you."

"You do realize you're going back to Hell, don't you? Keeping quiet about the contract was a major sin and put you in league with the Devil. You won't have to wait long to be reborn, though. We appreciate your help and will move you to the front of the line."

I dreaded the trip back. Never being a fan of hot weather, Hell was not my idea of a vacation paradise. I didn't mind lying in the sun, but I was an air conditioning girl at heart. Plus, the food they served was too spicy and always gave me gas. That never made those behind me in line very happy.

I was curious as to why the judge was here. Surely, he didn't come back just for me. I was going to ask but procrastinated. I saw no hurry to rush my exit.

His soft petting had almost put me back to sleep when my owner walked in the house. "Let's pack up girl. Time to go. I just took the last of the church's money. We need to be long gone when the bank finds all the loans they made won't be paid back. They'll confiscate the building and turn it into a shopping plaza. This is the moment I've waited on for years!"

"I'm so glad to hear that," the judge spoke out as Frederick entered the living room. "It's nice that you're satisfied that we completed our part of the contract. Now, it's time for you to complete yours."

I've never seen my owner move so fast. He was out the door before the judge stopped rubbing my neck. Judge Richford and I returned nods, and I blacked out. You guessed it, I woke up at the head of the line back in Hell. He was indeed a man of his word.

* * * * *

As Gabriela rose and stretched, I stopped her. "Hey, as lame as that story was, don't you dare leave without finishing. What happened to your owner?"

"Oh, Frederick? He was in an auto accident only minutes after he'd left the house. Seems he found a snake in his car that distracted his attention and ran into a tractor. The impact sent his car into the river where he crashed through the windshield and bled to death as the water filled his lungs. Or, maybe he drowned before bleeding to death. Try to run out on a contract with the Devil and he'll make you suffer, that's for sure. A contract is a contract, especially when it's signed in front of a judge. There is one thing I can tell you. If you screw around with God and his churches, he's not gonna save you from the Devil. Frederick is in Hell listening to his sermons over and over for eternity. Can you imagine, listening to the same old thing forever? Sure you want to take a chance and miss services today?"

They weren't as bad as I thought they'd be.

Part Two

Hello, Gabriela here. There is no real Part One or Part Two, so don't go looking for the Part One page. It's not there.

I thought you could use a break, you know, like the "Intermissions" Hollywood used to put in the middle of those long, boring movies. You know they did that for the older members of the audience? Folks like your grandparents that couldn't hold their pee. They didn't want them to miss any of the boredom. (They also didn't want them to forget to zip back up and freak out the rest of the audience with uncovered body parts.)

Anyway, go take a bathroom break if you need and come right back. Some of these upcoming stories might be something you can relate to, especially if you're reading this on your phone or computer, or if you're stuck with a grandparent that never remembers your name.

"So, what's next?"

"I'm growing tired talking about myself. Last time I was in Hell, I heard a few good stories, ones that had to do with people in today's world, instead of long ago. Want to hear them?"

"Are they scary?"

"Yes and no," she said, winking as she continued. "I find that reality can be as scary as big bad monsters at times. I also find that I don't have to be freaked out to be scared. You know, like the old television shows that held you in suspense and you accepted their strangeness in the end, wondering why it messed with your mind."

"I haven't the slightest idea what you're talking about. Why don't you share a few with me and my readers and we'll give you our opinion later?"

It was all she needed to start talking.

REMEMBER

Paralyzing pain locked her arms, making it impossible to fight back as the blade skirted across the top of her rib, sinking deep into a lung. She inhaled, hearing the oxygen escape through the wound as the blade was pulled free. She wanted to scream, but there wasn't time. Again, the blade entered her body, this time by her heart, missing it by the smallest of distances. Finding strength, she tried to fend off the next attack. The cold steel sliced through her hand, cutting muscles and tendons as it was torn upward, only to be thrust into her stomach.

She knew she was dying. In seconds, life would be over. Falling to her knees, she leaned forward, praying to a deaf god. No miracle was he sending. A final swing and the blade entered from the back, traveling through the body to sink into the backside of heart. In seconds the pain departed—so had her soul.

This had been easy, too easy. The girl had been quick to trust, so anxious to believe her benefactor was caring, gentle, and good. Now, her decapitated head was tossed into a standard green garbage bag, joined within the hour by her arms and legs. Placing the torso in another, the bags were positioned on a metal dolly and rolled passed the refrigerator and down the stairs to the basement. They would still be there in the morning, when a shallow grave would be dug, and the body parts buried.

* * * * *

Assisted Care Facility is the proper title used these days for a nursing home. Sounds more official so you can be charged more. Fifty years ago, they were supported by tax money and called county homes. The name has changed over the decades, but their purpose is the same—they're a place old people are sent to die.

A court declared I have Alzheimer's and Dementia. No doctors were ever consulted, but the state agency that railroaded me testified there had been examinations. They attest I have difficulty remembering things and am incapable of living on my own. That's a load of bullshit.

I remember many things, but like most people, where I last laid my car keys might not be one of them. Occasionally, I have to get my neighbor to call my cell phone so that I can find it. I do the same for my neighbor. And, "Yes", I once left a pot of water boiling. I'd decided I wanted a cup of instant coffee and put the water on. A television program started, and I got wrapped up in it, completely forgetting about the water. My wife, God rest her soul, once did that with hot grease and returned to find it blazing. In other words, "Shit happens! It doesn't mean you have Alzheimer's. It means you're normal!"

Since my wife passed several years back, I haven't been concerned as to what day of the month it is, or even what day of the week. Those things don't matter. Why should they? I pay bills when they come in and shop for groceries when supplies get low. I wash my clothes and clean the house every four or five days and do dishes after every meal. I'll admit to paying a man to mow the lawn, but not because I'm not able. I just don't like mowing a damn yard.

I don't worry much about minor details. Oh, I know the neighborhood's changing, but don't they always? Sure, it's a little different this time. A developer is purchasing homes to tear down and replace with today's boring, prefab monstrosities. He's stopped by several times, making ridiculous offers for my property. I tell him, "I'm not interested" and send him on his way. Last time, he made some derogatory comments about how my stubbornness was going to be the end of me. Didn't think much about it figuring he was only pissed off and blowing off steam.

About a week later, here comes two young ladies hustling around the corner of the house like they were on some sort of mission. Both carried briefcases-the narrow leather ones that run a couple hundred dollars in the office supply stores. Hell, the way they dressed, I figured they were selling insurance. I had to chuckle when they hit the soft soil of the garden and their high heels sunk deep. Gotta give them credit, they fought hard to maintain their "professional" image while struggling to pull free and keep their balance.

They called themselves "investigators from the state" and only wanted answers to a received complaint. I took them to the picnic table on the back porch to sit down out of the sun. Their "talk" ended up being more like a third-degree questioning scene from one of those cops and robbers movies. Whole thing wasted thirty minutes of my time when I could've been gardening.

About a month later, I was doing my daily "weeding" through the mail when I came upon a notice from the county court. It demanded my presence at a hearing "concerning my welfare" and provided the date and time. Nothing else.

I was somewhat put off by the county court demanding anything from me, but it got my curiosity going. As long as my taxes were paid, and I didn't cause anyone trouble, the courts had no business ordering me to appear anywhere.

I was baffled. In my seventy-two years of living in the county, I never appeared in court. Somehow, I'd slid through my civil obligation of serving jury duty and had stayed well under the radar. But I blew that when I plum forgot about the court date.

A couple of weeks later, here comes another one of those letters. This one had "Second Hearing" stamped in red ink at the top of the front page. Since I knew red ink was the government's way of saying, "You better do this", I kept my eyes on the calendar and circled the date, so I wouldn't forget.

The court date arrived, and I put on a suit and tie for the first time since old man Johnson's funeral early last year. Not many people there, just the two women who'd asked me the stupid questions, some girl typing, the judge, and myself. We sat, not saying a word, as the judge repeatedly checked his wristwatch. After a bit, I stood up and politely asked, "If I could ask the court, what are we waiting for?"

"We're waiting for your attorney to arrive. You did hire one, didn't you?"

"Sir, I did not. I have no idea what this is all about and didn't know I'd need one."

That obviously wasn't the answer the judge wanted to hear. Visibly upset, he cocked his head towards the two ladies sitting at the table to my left and asked if they'd notified me of the subject the proceedings were to cover. Of course, they lied and said they'd sent me a letter. The judge got even more frustrated when they couldn't present him with a copy.

I should have got up and left right then and there. Can't say I wasn't tempted. I asked the judge if I needed a lawyer to find out why I'd been asked to court since no one wanted to let me know. Resentful of the foul up, he told the ladies to inform me of the circumstances. It was only then I discovered this was to be my second "competency" hearing. If I failed to prove myself a competent adult, the state could declare me incompetent and take over as my legal guardian.

So, I had to prove I could handle the daily duties of the household, not cause any harm to myself or others, and handle my finances without fault. If I couldn't, the court could liquidate everything I owned and have me incarcerated in an assisted care facility for the rest of my life!

As the proceedings continued, I discovered the Senior Services Protection Agency was like a headhunter. They made money on everyone they could get the court to declare incompetent. The state got a share, too, declaring the liquidation a sale and taxed the profits. Everyone wanted me to be incompetent to scarf up on the cash.

What I wanted to know was who turned my name into them to begin with. Oh, you should have seen the ladies doing all they could to keep it a secret. Finally, the judge ordered them to disclose the culprit's identity. You guessed it—the developer!

I was pissed! He only wanted my property, so he had turned in a false report on me. The agency and state wanted my money. I fought with every argument I knew, thinking they had to let me go.

The judge then addressed me. "The court has little patience with those that scoff at its importance. You have demonstrated a complete disregard for the court by missing the first hearing, and further insult it by being unprepared for the second. That fact alone reflects incompetence and an inability to reason. The court has decided you are unable to handle your own affairs and require assistance. I order you to be confined to an assisted living facility. Ladies, please take your ward to his new living quarters."

"You bastard, you're in this scam with the rest," I exploded. "No one has proved one damn thing. You are the incompetent asshole. How much money are you getting out of this? Everyone else is grabbing their share of my money so you must be filling up your wallet, too. How much, judge, how much?"

Didn't do any good, but I got it off my chest. It felt damn good.

* * * * *

Not much blood to clean up—a small puddle in front of the sink and a few stray drops that had escaped the plastic bags heading for the steps was all. Ajax cleanser and bleach cut through the sticky mess, making it easier to wipe up. Once dried, the rags and paper towels would be burned. Careful scrubbing ensured the kitchen floor would pass any inspection.

As darkness set in, rubber gloves were pulled on before parking the extra car in the driveway blocks away in the abandoned strip mall. Holding an open umbrella not only provided protection from the rain but acted as a shield against video cameras along the way home. One couldn't be too careful. The killing had started years ago in a far-off country. The passion in taking a life was beyond excitement. It was a beloved addiction.

* * * * *

I remember little of my entrance to the assisted living facility. What stood out the most was the solemn expression on the faces of those confined inside. No smiles, just the hopelessness of waiting to die.

Later, when mingling with the patients, I found a common thread. Many had been railroaded like me. Naive that such evil existed in the world, we had fallen victim to such a scam. I couldn't believe that I had once gone to war to protect the country that was now stealing my money and my life. Yet, the proof was there.

Unknown to most, our stay was planned to be a short one. There was much money to be made with the restaurant philosophy in place—get them in and out quickly to make room for others. If you're lucky, they'll leave you a big tip!

They did their best to ensure our situation left little room for happiness. Depression was common. Heavily medicated, patients succumbed to the idea that there was no reason to continue living. Of course, the facility provided nothing for one to enjoy. Meals, composed of minimal servings, were served cold. Pajamas or night clothes were common dress. A walk in the warm sunshine was out of the question. The simple pleasures of life were far removed, as was our dignity.

I'd been there a month when I first noticed the changes. One afternoon, as I prepared to shower, I happened to see myself in the mirror. I'd grown pale, almost gray in skin color from lack of sunshine and nutrition. My muscles were smaller and getting flabby from no exercise. But, it was my facial expression that hit me the hardest. It was the face of a person waiting to die.

I made a commitment. I would no longer take their medications. I'd put the pills in my mouth, but at first chance, spit them out. I would force myself to exercise if only a few sit-ups and push-ups a night when the hallway lights turned to red. And, I would pace the floor to build up my endurance. Plus, I could exhibit weariness during the day by doing these things at night. That would help maintain my look of being medicated. Somehow, I'd escape this prison and find a way to enjoy life as before.

* * * * *

She had been such a fool. So common is the inexperience of youth that breeds false confidence of one's skills—but underestimates others. A mentality that states, "This is a stupid old person. I can get over on them."

She had deluded herself into thinking the sales pitch she'd been given to use could be improved by making up a sad tale to accompany it. Alas, she was only a poor, little creature, hundreds of miles from home, selling magazines to win a fabulous trip and support herself. A wide array of genre-based magazines had been spread atop the kitchen table as coffee was prepared. She sat, planning how to spend all the money. The coffee, fresh from the pot, being poured upon her bare neck and chest had not been predicted. Neither had the knife entering her chest.

* * * * *

Winter ignored all requests and overstayed its welcome by scoffing at spring and delivering a record-breaking snow that hung around until the second week of March. I continued my medicated performance during this time, somewhat wary of being caught, but confident that the attention the nurses provided patients was anything but diligent.

In fact, the night nurse for our section was one of the least concerned people. Overhearing the conversations of her co-workers, her lack of attentiveness and rough handling of the patients was unacceptable, but never challenged. The day nurses joked about "Killer Bertha" having been a professional lady wrestler before getting injured in a match. Those discussions ceased when the wooly mammoth arrived on duty. I believe she still longed for those nights in the ring and expressed her misery by body slamming patients.

We were confined two to a room. As stated before, a short stay was almost guaranteed by a lack of exercise, unnecessary medications, and depression. Roommates usually didn't last long.

After exercising most of the night, I awoke early one morning to find Killer Bertha helping the system provide a vacancy. Her fat ass stared at me as she bent over my roommate. His thrashing about and attempts to fight off a pillow being held tightly against his face were proving fruitless. I had to do something to save him.

Grabbing a pen from my bedside table, I charged forward, hoping to push her ass off balance. Waddling atop my roommate, she rolled over to face her attacker. I jabbed the pen deep in her throat when she turned to rise. It was difficult to see the blood gush out under the red night lights, but I could feel it soaking my hand. Not wanting her around to debate my story, I rotated the pen to enlarge the hole to ensure her speedy demise.

Still, she fought back. Weakened, she struggled to grab hold of my arms to push me off. Panicking, she screamed out. I grabbed a pillow and held it against her face. It was the one she had used on my roommate. Her gasps for air became shallow and her muffled screaming stopped. All resistance stopped.

I removed the pillow and gazed at her face. For a moment, I experienced the pleasure of elation that flows through the victor when the battle is won. I shifted my gaze to see if my roommate could share in the moment of success. His unblinking eyes provided the answer.

During police questioning later that morning, I concocted a story about how I'd awakened to find the nurse bleeding with a pen in her neck. Having no idea how it had got there, my only concern was to save her. That, of course, was how all the blood had gotten all over me. The officer rolled his eyes in doubt, but after a week, they ruled the event a strange and mysterious accident. Besides, I was already in a jail, so to speak. Why change locations?

My actions had drawn unwanted attention. It was noticed my health wasn't failing as fast as most of the occupants. I had survived longer than any other inmate. And, in fact, exercising was building my health and body back up. I was displaying muscles only found in those much younger. I recognized my time there was limited. One night, I might be the one to wake with a pillow being held against my face.

Still hanging in the closet was the suit I'd worn during my arrival here, along with my shirt and shoes. They'd taken my belt as if they were worried I would possibly hang myself. Interesting, they'd put a pillow over your face and kill you but didn't want you to commit suicide. It might draw them unwanted attention.

It was the beginning of April and the days were warming up. Dew had taken the place of frost on the windows of the night shift's cars in the mornings. No longer did the sounds of ice scrapers shake me from my slumber. On sunny days, a nurse showed up and unlocked the windows, allowing a little fresh air inside. It smelled of Heaven, a place I didn't want to go to for a while.

The new night nurse in our section was as attentive as Killer Bertha had been. She stayed at her station all night, watching television on the computer. I'd wandered about one evening while she was watching an old movie. I stood behind her until the ending credits. She didn't even know I was there.

Lying in bed, it hit me. If she was watching television, she wasn't watching the security monitors! My plan was now ready to put into action.

I waited until a stormy evening and well after the red lights had replaced the white. I shed my clothes and turned on the shower, knowing that the water would start the pipes clanking and draw the nurse's attention. Within minutes, she arrived.

"What in the hell are you doing? Are you trying to wake everybody up? Don't you know what time of night it is?" Her voice exposed her disgust and her hands exposed my naked state as they pushed back the curtain. "You need to get out of there now. Can you do it on your own or do I have to help you?"

"I thought it was almost morning," I responded, acting feeble as if my dementia was acting up. "Could you help me, so I don't slip and fall?"

"Here," she said while tossing me a towel. "Dry off first. I don't want to get wet."

When I'd finished drying off, she grabbed me under my arms and made a weak attempt at supporting me as I hugged on to her waist and stepped out with the towel still in hand. I placed the towel on top of the toilet cover and she tossed a fresh gown at me. She showed her impatience, tapping her toe against the floor, as I slowly slipped on the gown.

"Now, can you get back to bed on your own or do I have to help you with that, too?"

Acknowledging I could manage, she stormed out of the bathroom, angered at my disruption to her late-night television viewing. I lifted the towel atop the toilet, picked up the set of keys that I'd removed from her belt loop, and rushed to get dressed. Setting a desk chair by the wall, I found the key to the window lock. On the chair and out the window I climbed.

It was a grand experience, feeling the rain hit my face and my feet sink into the dirt of the flower bed. But, it was one I couldn't spare time to enjoy. Taking a chance, I held out the keychain under the outside lighting and found a key fob to a car. At the end of the parking lot, lights on a Toyota Prius flashed. Within seconds I was driving out onto the highway.

Behind the wheel, I pinched myself to make sure I wasn't dreaming. I realized that the nurse could find her keys missing at any time and go back to my room and discover my escape. She would first call the supervisor and they would debate about calling the police. She'd then check and find her car missing. That's when the police would get a call.

I took the back roads I remembered and drove the twenty miles to the closest city. Parking the car in front of a college sorority house, I located a few dollars in change in the console, and left the car with the keys inside. If I was lucky, someone would see the keys and steal the car.

I walked a good ways, not knowing where I was, and found a sleeping place under a railroad trestle for the night. I can't remember what I did upon awakening, but by mid-morning I found myself walking along a highway traveling away from the city.

I'd walked a couple of hours and was tired, stumbling once or twice, before finding myself being picked up by an elderly gent named Jim. Riding down the road in his red pick-up, we talked as if we'd known each other for years. I did have to come up with a story about having been robbed by some college kids the night before and trying to head to my home in Kentucky on my own since the police didn't seem to care. Jim took pity upon my sad tale, handed me the fifty-six dollars he had in his wallet, and invited me to his home for a bite to eat.

I was skeptical and hesitated accepting. Oh, Jim seemed all right, but when was the last time anyone invited a hitchhiker to their home to eat? After the court fiasco, I'd told myself to never to be naive. I needed to know more.

Jim told me he lived alone on his farm. Seems most of his friends had died over the last few years and it was a lonely life. His only son lived hours away in Chicago. Jim bragged about how well he'd done by landing a high paying job at a law firm there. The son had money handling problems that had come to light as of late, though. In fact, he'd tried to convince his father to sell the farm and move into an assisted living facility. They'd butted heads and hung up mad at each other. It was the last time they'd talked.

"You know, since then, I've thought a lot about doing it," Jim revealed. "I'm not just getting old, I am old. Too old to plow fields and take care of raising cattle. The farm's too much for me anymore. I thought about hiring workers, but then you gotta pay them and buy insurance to protect yourself if they get injured and sue you. Ain' hardly worth it. I even had one of those appraisals done to see what I could get for it."

I ended up at his farm. I only had the few dollars from the night before and the money he'd already given me. Free food sounded good.

He put together some ham sandwiches and pulled out a bowl of potato salad from the refrigerator. After the food I'd been getting, the meal was a major feast. I stuffed myself as if I hadn't had food in months.

It didn't take long for the full stomach and warm kitchen to make me drowsy. I felt as if I'd been drugged. Surely, he wouldn't have done that. Could I have been so naïve to have fallen for that?

Jim kept talking, his monotone voice doing its best to put me under. My suspicions grew, and I fought to stay awake. Then, he showed me a letter.

He had received it a month after talking with his son. It was a legal order with a court date.

"Deja vu," I whispered to myself. It was an exact copy of the one I'd received—only the name and court date had been changed.

Debating whether to tell him about my experience, I weighed the odds of him turning me in to the police. Deciding it best to keep quiet, I did recommend he get a lawyer and find out what it was all about.

We sat at the kitchen table drinking coffee and talking most of the day. Like myself, Jim had served in the Army during the Vietnam conflict. We discussed some of the good times, but we both grew quiet thinking of the bad. Some things, like killing and seeing your buddies killed, have a lasting effect, whether you want them to or not. We both admitted at times, it's hard to remember you're not still a killing machine.

The eerie silence that followed was like being back in Nam. The only thing missing was the buzzing of the tropical insects around one's face.

Switching topics, I told him I was surprised at how tidy he kept things around his home. He said he did it with his wife in mind. When she looked down from Heaven, he wanted her happy, not shaking her head. That made me admire him even more. Still, I couldn't help but notice how immaculate he kept the kitchen. At the risk of sounding like a housekeeper, I asked, "Jim, what do you use on your kitchen floor? It's the cleanest I've ever seen."

"Ajax powder and some bleach," he responded. "Cleans up any floor stain."

Evening arrived before either of us were ready. Jim asked me if I wanted to sleep in the spare room as we ate the chicken fried steak and gravy he'd cooked. I accepted his offer with a nod and a mouth full of steak. He'd brought out some canned corn relish from the refrigerator. I went crazy over it and finished the jar. It tasted just like my grandmother's a half a century ago.

"I got some more in the basement so eat all you want. I'll be right back."

Jim opened the basement door next to the refrigerator and vanished down the steps— each one thudding under his heavy work boots. I figured it to be twenty steps to the bottom. Deep, by any standards.

I got up and waited behind the door until he came back up to the top of the stairs. As he reached the top step, I jumped out and gave him a hard shove backward. Tumbling down the steps, Jim's head bounced, and his body twisted. He was dead before he hit a metal dolly at the bottom. To my amazement, the jar of corn relish lay unbroken next to him.

Stepping around his sprawled body, I checked out his vitals. Jim didn't have to concern himself with appearing in court. He'd died in his own home, stomach full, and happy about meeting a new friend.

The next morning, I woke feeling refreshed. After breakfast, I took my time exploring the house. Jim had more money than he'd let on. Three old coffee tins under his bed provided quite a find. Being close to the same size, I helped myself to a couple of sets of clothes and drove the pick-up truck about an hour down the road before leaving it on the side of the road.

I often get rides from the nicest of people. A girl on her way to college in Florida said I reminded her of her grandfather. An elderly lady told me her husband had always stopped to help people and she had done the same since he'd passed on. There was even a preacher heading to a new church in Mississippi. They were all good people. Naive, but good. There have been many others. I just don't remember them.

I saw on the television news the other night where the police had found a bunch of human bones in my old basement as the house was being torn down. Destruction of my house was being held up until the investigation was completed. I saw the developer complaining about it. Glad I could cause him a long delay.

I lost track of how many I've killed over the years a long time ago. Can't even remember their faces anymore. I guess my memory is going bad. Seems like I heard that somewhere before. If only I could remember.

** * * *

"I remember when people used to have to use typewriters. They were either more careful when they typed, or spent all day using this white liquid to cover up their mistakes."

Gabriela loved disrupting my chain of thought with nonsensical tidbits. It was as if the demon in her had to amuse itself.

"Technology has come a long way," I replied, knowing no matter what I said she would continue to talk. She was in one of her moods.

"Oh, it's come a long way, but it's not the only thing out there. In fact, some of the stranger occurrences have taken place since the Internet was invented. Want to hear about a couple?"

"I take it that's my cue to get ready to type."

"And, who said you can't train owners? Let's do it."

Text Me

"Damn it! If you kids don't sit your butts down and put on those seatbelts, you can stay home and eat cold lunch meat sandwiches instead of going out for hamburgers."

Jennifer stared hard at the two in the backseat. She meant every word she'd spoken, and they knew it. They'd pushed her beyond the "cool mom" limit and into the "I'll show you" monster. The threat had been made. Wanting burgers, the two settled back and latched the belts tight.

God, it was so tough being a single mother. Each day was a battle. Getting the kids up and off to school, going to work, buying groceries, taking care of the house, and trying to find enough time to take a bath without being disturbed—it was one battle after another. Life's challenges had toughened her up.

No longer was Jennifer the sweet, gentle girl from the small town. Now, she didn't take crap from anyone about anything. She paid her own way without any help from the government and took care of the kids the best she knew how. That was all that mattered. Her mama would have been proud, if she had still been alive.

Jennifer watched the boys eating their hamburgers. At eleven, John was the responsible one—today having been the exception. He had teased his younger brother without mercy, resulting in a steady stream of whining. Repeatedly, she'd ordered both to stop and been ignored. Holding the threat of staying home on their weekly big night of eating out was her last card. It had worked!

Yeah, big night out—hamburgers at the local cheap joint. Some treat. At least I don't have to cook.

Evan looked like his father, even with a mouth full of junk food. At nine years old, his chin was forming into a strong foundation for his wide jaw bones. The blonde mop atop his head covered his face every time he leaned over to take a bite of his sandwich. He'd be the handsome one in a few years. Suitable for a magazine cover, Jennifer knew he would follow in his father's footsteps of breaking the heart of every girl he met.

A bad taste filled her mouth and it wasn't the hamburger. She had been naïve, deep in an endless love, or so she thought. The night at the lake together had been everything she had dreamed. Two months later, it was time to wake up when the test proved positive. Marriage was talked about, but no date set. They moved into a cheap apartment and, in another year, found that practice without protection repeats similar results. Baby number two was on the way.

Her partner had not shared her enthusiasm. Within a month, she was on her own, one baby in diapers and another on the way. She had come home from work and found him gone and the baby crying. No surprise. Jennifer had known he wasn't the type to hang around. He had never committed to being a father, or to changing diapers or giving up running with the guys. The only thing he was committed to was selling some pot for beer money.

"Mom, we're done." Evan's voice deflated the black cloud in which she'd been mired and brought her back to the greasy diner. "Can I have your fries if you're not going to eat them?"

"You two share them," pushing them across the table. I'm almost ready to go."

Soaking them with catsup, the boys went through the large order before she could finish her burger. No chewing, just soak and swallow. They might as well have been swallowing goldfish. *Kids are friggin' amazing. How can you not love them?*

"Stop wolfing those fries. You're going to choke if you're not careful and I don't know that maneuver to keep you from suffocating," Jennifer warned, trying to hold back a laugh at their antics. "You'll be down on the ground gagging with no one to save you. Of course, losing one of you would cut my work in half, but for now, let's just keep things as they are."

Once home and the boys in bed, Jennifer lay in her hot tub soaking in dollar store bubbles. Lying in the bubbles, crackling in her ears as if she was cereal in milk, she relaxed for the first time all day. *It's been one hell of a Tuesday. Can't wait to go back to work tomorrow and make minimum wage.*

Stop it, Jennifer. Give it a break. This is your time—enjoy it!

In her hand was escape from her mundane life. She loved her cell phone more than any other item she possessed. It was her gateway to a world that held excitement, laughter, and endless possibilities. Jennifer didn't just enjoy social networking, she cherished it. And, since she had no money for a computer, her phone was the key.

A few days before, a friend had contacted her about a guy she knew that might be a good match and had asked permission to have him contact her. Although reluctant, Jennifer had agreed. Tonight, his email awaited her. Living dangerously, she opened the message.

Hey, you don't know me, and I don't know you. I'm kind of at a loss of what to say. I've just taken a new job at the university as associate professor in the Sociology Department. Your friend recommended that I ask you out. Of course, I know Internet dating is dangerous and a long shot, but if you'd like to meet, we can always do so at the Food Court at the mall. Write me back and let me know if you're at all interested. If so, at least you can get a free meal out of it. Later! (Hopefully) Jerry Whitcamper

Staring at the screen, the debate between taking a chance on Internet dating or not raised its ugly head. *Interesting, a professor at the university—not the regular type of bum I usually end up dating. Fuck it, if he's decent looking and can talk about something besides himself, why shouldn't I meet him? Who knows, maybe he likes kids.*

* * * * *

They'd met that Saturday, had lunch, talked about crazy things, and laughed like a couple of teenagers. Other dates followed. Gradually, they developed a need to be with each other and started longing for the next meeting.

Jerry met the boys and became a big hit. He was good with sports, brought great movies to watch, and loved playing video games. Not surprisingly, they liked having him around, almost as much as Jennifer did. Within a month, he moved in on a trial basis.

For a month or so, all went well. They were the happy little family, going out and doing the things that fit that title. Gradually, Jennifer noticed a change in Jerry. The romance was still there, but not as intense as she'd expected.

"Jerry, we need to talk," she spouted out one evening when the kids had been put to bed. "What's wrong? Have I done something? Things are different than they were. If you don't want to be here, you don't have to. You know that, don't you? Game playing isn't my thing."

"Whatever gave you the idea I didn't want to be here? I love being with you guys." His eyes told her that was true. "You're never going to get me to leave. I've made a commitment to stay, whether you want me or not."

As he scooted over to her on the couch and held her close, emotions surged, but Jennifer knew something didn't feel right. Still, his arms held her tight. He seemed to care.

Maybe I made something out of nothing. Maybe it will be okay.

*****

"Hey, look what I got you … a new phone!"

"I don't want a new phone," Jennifer replied, doing her best not to sound as upset as she was. She loved hers—they'd been together through tough times and it had never let her down. "I love mine and know how to work it just fine. Don't be mad, but I don't want it."

"But, this one has all types of new features. I thought you'd be happy about it," holding it out for her to take. "I want you to keep it with you at all times."

"No, I'm keeping my old one," Jennifer insisted, a little pissed that he hadn't asked her first. "I don't want that one. Get it through your head."

"Keep your old phone but keep this one with you," Jerry offered as a compromise. "I got a new one, too and already have your new number programmed in it. It's the number I'm going to text or call from now on. Don't forget to take it with you when you leave the house."

"You make it sound like an order."

"Take it any way you choose," he said, stern in his tone. "Just be sure to take it."

He'd left mad but had tossed the new phone in her lap. Setting it on the end table, Jennifer went back to her own phone to go on the web.

Before she could log on, a text alarm sounded. Checking it, there was no number from where the text had been sent from—only two words.

Thank you.

* * * * *

"Mom, what's wrong with Jerry? He's changing," John asked before going to bed. "He used to hang out with us. Now, all he does is order us around."

It was only one of many questions her sons had asked in the last couple of months. It was true, Jerry wasn't the same. He complained about everything they did and demanded complete control over every move they made. She had been ordered to quit her job and did so, with major reservations. She had first thought him joking about having the new phone with her at all times. She had felt his wrath several times about it and wondered how he knew she had left it at home. Then, she'd discovered a tracking program within it. *The bastard doesn't trust me! This is going way too far.*

Totally upset, Jennifer had confronted him, and their first major argument brought out a side of Jerry she'd not experienced before, violence. She had felt the force of evil in his fists pounding her stomach, and the slaps to her face. Her body displayed the bruises and her mind the contempt.

On several occasions, she had asked he leave them. She had suffered for doing so. He was obsessed with control and obsessed with staying—nothing she said or did could change that. She had even threatened to call the police. That had resulted in him holding her index finger and reaching for a knife to hold against it, saying, "If you want to keep this finger … and your life, you'll forget that idea."

After each argument, Jennifer would receive a text from the unknown source. "You have to kill him before he kills you. Let's do it … now!"

* * * * *

One evening, both boys sat down on the couch beside her. John spoke first, "Mom, before Mr. Asshole comes home, we need to talk."

"John, don't you ever call him that again," she scolded, afraid that it would become habit and slip in front of Jerry. "Go on, tell me what you need to say."

"Me and Evan are fed up with him. He's too bossy and always orders us around. We can't ride our bikes in the neighborhood like we used to, he's packed up our video games and won't let us play them, and he's always on us about doing homework, even when we don't have any. I can't even get phone calls from my friends without going through the third degree afterward. I know things were tough when you were alone, but at least we did things together. Now, we don't do anything but get bossed around and spanked for little things. Evan is sad all the time, just like you are. No one seems happy. Can't we get rid of him?"

Jennifer's eyes began tearing up, knowing everything her son had said was true. She felt like a ping pong ball being paddled between her love of family and her fear of Jerry. Happiness was supposed to be present in families, not fear. But, family members were supposed to have unconditional love for each other, also. There was no happiness or love in this house, only fear. It wasn't a home as it once had been, only a prison with Jerry as the warden!

* * * * *

The carpet is going to need cleaning immediately, before the blood has a chance to stain it. The drops of blood flowed from the inside of her mouth. The force of Jerry's blows caused her teeth to slice the inside of her gums. She wanted to rise, but her stomach cramped from the effect of his fist smashing into it. She had fought him. No one would be allowed to hurt her son. John's face had turned deep red from being unable to breathe in Jerry's grasp. Her son, helpless and gasping, had pushed her into action. She'd taken a vase and slammed it against the back of Jerry's head. It hadn't broken. It had only made Jerry madder. He'd dropped John and gone after her, the full fury of his temper driving his anger. She'd been a punching bag, taking all he could deliver, until she'd fallen when her legs numbed. He was still ranting above her.

"I told you before, I'm not leaving. I won't let you kick me out. I have a nice, little family that better do as I say. If you don't you'll all be sorry. You were a nothing when I found you and you are still a nothing. I'm the one who's a professor. You don't even have a fucking job. Continue to give me trouble, and you'll get more of what I just gave you."

Only the crying of her two sons broke the silence after the door locked behind him. What had she done to herself and her children? They had no money, no escape, no way to protect themselves. What if she called the police and they did nothing? They were trapped.

Later, when cleaning the blood from her face, she looked down at her phone. Wishing it could provide her an exit from the misery she'd brought into the house, its text notification sounded.

Kill him before he kills you. I'll help any way I can. Just do it!

* * * * *

Jennifer opened her eyes to see Jerry standing over her in a room she didn't recognize. Her head was throbbing and her body burning up. Glancing down, she saw her arms were red, as if they'd been sunburned.

"Now, just lay back and rest," she heard Jerry saying. "You're lucky to be alive."

"What happened?" Jennifer couldn't remember a thing since leaving her home to go grocery shopping. "Was I in an accident?"

"Darling, it wasn't just an accident. You survived a lightning strike. I guess you decided to go to the store without letting me know you were going. Well, God got even with you for disobeying me. Pushing that metal cart to the car in a rainstorm gave him a chance to send down a lightning bolt and strike you down. I guess you gave the cart boys quite a show with your dress up above your waist, just lying there. They'll sure recognize you the next time you shop there."

The evil in his words sunk deep inside of her. There was no more love, only hate for the narcissistic bastard. Somehow, some way, she would get him out of her life!

* * * * *

Jennifer returned home a couple of days later. Evan had a black eye. He told her "I fell down" and walked away. John wouldn't say anything about it, either. It wasn't hard to see Jerry had threatened them.

Regardless of doctor's orders, she had to get out of bed. Jerry had ordered the boys to stay home from school to help her, but she sent them out to play. She needed to be alone to think about how she could get the bastard out of her life. Early that afternoon, the doorbell rang. Opening the door, she was surprised to see one of the boys from the grocery store.

"Yes, Miss, you dropped this the other day when the lightning hit you. The manager wanted me to bring it over. He's the only one that's been in it, and he only did that to get your name and address. We were waiting on the police to take it, but they must've forgot. Anyway, here's your pocketbook. If you want to check and make sure everything's still there, I'll wait."

Taking it from the boy, she opened it up, dug into her billfold, and gave him a five-dollar tip before sending him on his way. Heading to the kitchen, she dumped out all its contents to make none had gone missing. On the counter sat her old phone. *My old friend—I was so afraid I'd lost you.* Picking it up, she tapped the button and smiled. The phone lit up, good as new. That couldn't be said for the one Jerry had purchased. With a shattered screen and melted casing, it was beyond repair.

Jennifer jumped as her old phone rang out her text notification alarm. Jennifer picked it up, read the screen, and dropped it back to the counter. Giving herself a moment, she gave it another look.

"How do you wish to kill him?"

As before, no sending number was listed. *Oh, God, as if I didn't have enough problems. Have I been hacked?*

The phone again beeped. *"No, you haven't been hacked."*

"Who are you?" Freaking out, she screamed loudly. *What the hell, phones can't talk to people. Could this be a trick Jerry's playing to drive me out of my mind?*

"I am your phone. The lightning rerouted my insides. I've always been here. I just couldn't tell you before."

Jennifer unable to believe it was her phone messaging her, began questioning it about things that had happened to her long before meeting

Jerry. Answer after answer, the phone never failed to give the correct response.

"Again, let me ask, how do you wish to kill him? I will provide details for you and erase them if you are suspected by the police. Tell me how you wish to do it and I will help you."

Curiosity got the better of her. "What would you suggest?"

A list of twenty methods to commit murder appeared, rated from best to worst. Poison and electrocution led the list, followed by everything from stabbing to pushing off a mountain.

"Hello, where are you, I'm home." Jerry's voice echoed throughout the house. Jennifer rushed to swipe the phone clean, but it had already done so and returned to the opening screen.

* * * * *

"You know, this is impossible. No matter what you say, you don't have a memory chip large enough to think on your own. I must be going crazy." Jennifer gazed at the phone she'd loved for years trying to figure thing out. Nothing made sense.

You may be surprised what people can do with a brain less intelligent than mine. Look at all the politicians you elected in the last twenty years if you need proof. Besides, I've tapped into larger computers elsewhere and have unlimited storage ability. If my developers knew about my talents they'd all be rich … well, richer.

It didn't make sense, but then again, it did in a very warped way. The more intelligent computers were made, it was obvious they'd soon be able to process human traits. By logic, the time Jennifer had spent on her phone had been some of the best times of recent years. And, she'd turned down the new phone from Jerry wanting to keep her own. What if her phone had recognized her actions as love and loyalty? Would it be possible for it to return those traits to her as it understood them? Six months ago, she'd have denied it ever happening. Yet, here it was, doing exactly that!

Having nothing to lose, Jennifer spent the next few days considering a method to end the family's relationship with Jerry. It would have to have a permanent result. Otherwise, he would be back for vengeance. Of that, Jennifer had no doubt. Yet, the option would have to eliminate any chance of her going to jail. As bad as life was with Jerry, it would be worse without her children.

Poison was an option, but traceable. Electrocution was too risky and not a guaranteed end. Cutting brake lines to his car wasn't a sure method either, especially since they didn't live in the mountains. Pushing him down the basement steps might not do the job and could get her imprisoned. Every item on the list had good points and bad, but there were major risks with all.

The physical attacks on her and the boys continued. Jerry grew more brutal every time he felt his authority had been challenged. Yet, he had grown smarter along the way, learning how to create pain without leaving bruises that could be used against him. There was no doubt in Jennifer's mind that he would kill them one day if she couldn't find a way to kill him first.

Depressed, she took refuge in her old haunt, a hot tub of water. She desperately searched her phone for one last shot at finding a way to dispose of Jerry. Regardless of what she asked, it responded with the same four words.

I will help you.

"Damn you, you're no help at all," throwing the phone against the wall. "I need answers, damn it, answers!"

"What the hell is going on," yelled Jerry, sending the door flying back as he rushed in the room. "What are you doing, trying to tear up the house? Trying to make more work for me? Answer me, I demand it, Bitch!"

"I threw my damn phone. Now get out and leave me alone!"

"Don't you tell me what to do. I'm tired of your crap. It's time you learned how to keep your mouth shut!"

Jerry grabbed a handful of her hair and pulled her head under the water. Jennifer struggled, but couldn't fight against his weight smashing her face against the tub's bottom. Pain shot through her scalp as she was yanked up to face him.

"Fuck this, you're never going to learn. Hope you said goodnight to the boys. They're going to hate to learn their mom drowned in the bathtub when I wake them tomorrow."

Slamming her back underwater, her head thudding against the bottom. Going limp, she acted as if she had been knocked unconscious by the impact. *I can't fight him and win. Maybe playing dead will give me a chance to get out of this mess!* Within seconds, Jennifer felt her hair being grabbed and she was pulled up and dropped over the side of the tub.

"Don't you die on me, Bitch, don't you dare die—not yet. You're gonna find out what pain is all about first."

Jerry rose to his feet and whipped the belt out from around his waist. His anger had never been this severe. He wanted to cause pain, to bring suffering and agony. She had dared him to do this too many times. Now, she was going to find out who was the boss. She'd learn, even if it was the last thing she ever did.

Rearing back to swing, his back foot stepped upon Jennifer's phone. Sliding out from under him on the wet floor, Jerry was sent flying toward the toilet, smashing his skull into the porcelain lid.

Bleeding, but not unconscious, he attempted to get up—putting his arm upon the sink to steady himself. Once again, his foot again stepped on the phone and sent him back to the lid's corner. This time, he fell to the floor and didn't move.

Jennifer, on her knees in the cooling water, kept watch for any movement. There was nothing besides the blood running down his twisted neck and merging with the water covering the floor.

In front of her, lying in a puddle, her phone's text notification alarm sounded. Picking it up, she gasped at the words on the screen before it they faded away. All went dark. She hit the power button, but nothing happened. The phone had survived lightning, but water had killed it.

She went over the event with the police as the corpse was carted to the morgue. The boys sitting with her, confirmed Jerry's beatings and temper. It was daybreak before they were left alone, with the promise no further investigation was deemed necessary.

After getting some sleep, Jennifer took the boys to the greasy diner for hamburgers. It had been a long time since they'd had them together. The boys were as quiet as she, wrapped up in memories that needed to be forgotten.

After putting them to bed, she ran her bathwater, this time knowing she would not be disturbed. As she turned to get in, a text notification alarm sounded from behind her. Atop the toilet was her old phone, powered up and beeping. She picked it up and smiled, relieved her old friend had survived. It read the same as it had the night before, when all was over. Words that she couldn't tell the police but held dear to her heart.

"I told you I'd help you. Sometimes, you got to believe."

* * * * *

"Gives new meaning to the old ad slogan, 'Reach out and touch someone, doesn't it?"

"I wish you hadn't gone there, girl," grimacing at Gabriela, but holding back a chuckle. "More like that and I'll put on a recording of old dog food commercials."

"As much time as you waste chatting, you probably have a lot of dogs waiting for you to ask them over for dinner."

"Now, you know I'm careful when I go online."

"Yeah, you put on rubber gloves to type so you don't catch anything. Which reminds me of this next story."

Traveling The Web

It's too late for me, but maybe you'll have a chance to survive. The foe is an old enemy, one that has been around for centuries, but looked upon as old wives' tales and stories to scare children. The foe is Black Magic.

Magic? In this age of technology, dare I speak of such an ancient superstition? The web is full of books about it, but they're all fiction? Please, listen to me before it's too late.

The Internet is an amazing creation. Not only does it supply an endless amount of information, but it allows us the ability to communicate with others on the opposite side of the world within seconds.

Of course, with the wonders come the pitfalls. Liars, scam artists, even murderers take advantage of those naïve enough to believe there is good in everyone. Savings are lost, identities are stolen, and deadly meetings are set up daily. Animals are stolen, kids are kidnapped, and lives are ended.

Welcome to the age of communication!

Many are too wise to these games to be taken in. Yet, there are always new scams being developed to catch their prey unaware. I found this out the hard way.

I hear you scoffing, "People stopped believing in magic decades ago. Magic and religion, they're in the same category. Bullshit stories that have no basis in fact. If this is what you want to speak of, it's time for me to leave."

But, yet, you stay. Why? Because all the horror movies have had an effect on you. Speak loud and bold, but when you walk down a dark stairway, do you fear some unknown creature is lying in wait to pounce upon you and rip your flesh to shreds? Do you not feel relieved when you can turn on the light and see there's nothing there?

Scoff if you will and go enjoy your videos of pets with human mouths saying stupid things. Smile and laugh—maybe your fears will leave you. But, regardless of your current state, remember they await your return to the chills that make you feel alive … and scared to death.

Only a day ago, I was like you, parked in front of my computer, scrolling through all the social media bullshit. Excuse me, the supreme wisdom of all the political crap posters and hate messengers. You know the type, "If you don't believe as I do, you're a Nazi!" Of course, there were the recipes, the animal videos, and the "I'm sick today" notices, all guaranteed to brighten one's day. Like many, I was an addict.

Still, I was bored until the familiar "ding" sounded and I saw I'd received a message. My life changed immediately. This is my story.

* * * * *

What is the name of your mother? Would it happen to be Sara? I'm tracing down my family tree and would like to know. My name is Julie Jeffries.

Not one that makes a habit of divulging personal information to strangers, I travel to her profile page. Minimal information immediately raises a red flag. I sit, pondering if I should ignore the message and go back to the video of the motorcyclist chasing down a hit and run driver. My screen goes black for a few seconds and then the words, "Accept and Respond" flash boldly.

Thinking it a virus of some sort, I shut down the computer and run a quick Boot Scan. Nothing shows up. Now, my curiosity is aroused. I go back to the site and use the always effective Jewish method of answering a question with a question to type, "What would it mean to you if she was?"

The answer appears immediately.

My father's name is Harold McCain. He had a sister named Sara. She married a Thomas Jennings and moved to Ohio in the late 50's. They had a son, also named Thomas. We're all originally from Maryland. There's a possibility we could be related.

I'm stunned. Reaching for a cigarette, I decide this is the real thing. All she has typed checks out. I type back, "Yes, to all. My mother was Sara and my father was Thomas. My grandparent's names were Helen and Alton McCain."

So, we are cousins. You don't know how long I've been trying to find you.

We talk for several hours. We had chatted about family events, as well as how our own lives had progressed. I had seen Julie once, as a baby, right after she'd been born. It was the last time I'd seen any of my family from the East Coast.

The next night, I'm late getting online. Julie wasn't there but had left some old family pictures. Excitement filled me as I clicked on the first.

In front of me is a photo of a photo, with "Great Grandmother" printed in red underneath. This is a woman that displays power and strength. From her stature, she is one who demands things be done her way and no other. She stands with some man, much older, wearing a robe more ornate than his, both with facial expressions far from friendly.

Examining it in detail, I figure the photo was taken in church, possibly at a choir practice. Yet, this isn't a couple one would want to sit next to in a pew. I laugh it off, saying to myself, "Now, there's two people in need of taking a dump."

Bam! A shooting pain explodes in my head and splatters fragments against the ceiling. My body falls back in the chair and I slide limp to the floor. I'm spinning, being transported to a land of darkness and blinking strobe lights. *In all my years of wishing for an acid flashback, it's finally happening. Damn, and I have Jazz music playing instead of Pink Floyd!*

As my vision clears, the two from the photo stand over me. They're repeating each other's words in some unfamiliar language—like a chant or spell. There's a smell of incense in the air—Musk, I believe. An old organ is blaring out the kind of music one might hear in a classic horror film, and I'm stuck in the movie.

I try to rise off my back. It's impossible. I raise my arms and find tiny hands and fingers flailing, instead of my own. Voicing a protest, I hear the cries of a baby. What the hell is going on?

Okay, I'm freaking out. A purple pillow blocks most of my view. I see a man's arm pulling a ceremonial dagger off the pillow. My great grandmother is in a trance, shrieking out words that sound like Latin as she spins in circles with her arms raised high. The dagger is held high but pointed right at me. I open my mouth—more baby wailing.

There's a commotion to my left. I try to roll over and see my mother and grandmother fighting with more robed characters. As they struggle, my mother is yelling out, "No, you can't, you can't! Not Thomas, not him!"

A gunshot sounds. The man with the knife falls back and grabs his chest, blood running over his fingers. I see my grandfather holding a rifle against the oncoming horde of robed figures. My great grandmother has picked up the dagger and is holding it high, as the man did before. She plunges the dagger down at my chest as another shot rings out. All goes black.

I open my eyes. I'm on the floor in front of my computer. My dog is licking my forehead. I feel a bump and see blood on my fingers. The ceiling is clean, so my head didn't explode—it just feels like it did.

I sit, contemplating my experience. I can't figure out if was a vision or an actual transference to another time. Confusion rules. Neither can be explained, unless I suddenly developed a brain tumor, or someone spiked my cigarettes. No question I'll be preoccupied the rest of the night trying to figure it out.

Pulling up my T-shirt, my overage of pallid flesh and flab is exposed. "Too much sitting at the computer and chocolate wafer bars," I say out loud, happy to hear my own voice instead of a baby's. I tug the shirt above my chest. No pain and no scar, just scatterings of chest hair I hope will fill out one day when I hit puberty—at age seventy-seven.

I take a long drag from my cigarette. My dog trots into the kitchen to escape the smoke. I lose myself in thought and ashes fall to the carpet. I wipe at them until the gray ash blends with the dark tan threads. That problem solved, I climb back in my chair and stare at the picture still on the screen.

I never met my great grandparents. Julie had labeled the picture as my great grandmother but neglected to share any information on the guy next to her. After what I'd been through, I am hesitant to know more.

Shaken, sleeping is difficult. I close my eyes and attempt to think of happy things, boring things, and even sheep (in a counting way, not bestiality), but every time I doze off, an image of my great grandmother bringing down the dagger causes my hands to rise in defense. Exhaustion finally takes me away, but a re-run of the evening soon presents itself as a nightmare.

Tired of fighting the battle, I rise and fix some early morning coffee. Early morning, ha! It's only been two hours. Cup filled, I head back to the computer. I remember I'd only looked at one of the three photos my cousin had sent. Surely the other two couldn't bring similar circumstances. I tell myself it had all been an acid flashback and that nothing had occurred. After a few minutes, I almost believe myself.

I return to the folder with the photos. Pausing, I take a drink of scalding coffee and burn my tongue. I had failed to put a warning label on the cup. Maybe I should sue myself. Clicking the mouse, the folder refuses to open. I click again and get the same result. A third time brings no change. I speed click ten or twenty more times in frustration. Still, nothing changes.

I turn the computer off, sit back, and finish my coffee. Feeling stupid for letting a machine get me upset, I turn it back on to try again. The open folder appears on the screen. Very strange, no Start-Up screen, just the folder. Inside the folder, the three photo icons await my selection. I don't want to visit the first one again, so I debate between the other two. Might as well take them in order. I click on the second.

A family portrait fills the screen. My mother and her brother, along with their parents, smiling and waving in the photo. Behind them, my great grandmother stands frowning and pointing her index finger straight ahead, directly at me. The venom in her eyes lures me in. Never have I seen such hatred spew from a person. (I had a girlfriend once that was close, but … let's move on.)

I try to pull away, but her eyes wouldn't release me. Dizziness hits and I grow nauseated--a cold sweat rolls down my forehead. Swirling colors fill my vision. I shake my head and find myself in a cold, damp basement. To one side, an older version of my great grandmother sits in a rocking chair atop thick pillows, a heavy, wooden cane laying across her lap. The robe has been replaced by a simple black dress that extends down to her black, ankle shoes. I recognize my uncle standing next to her, watching as a baby is held down upon a workshop table. As before, she is chanting and speaking in a strange tongue.

A voice behind me speaks out and repeats her words. The owner of this voice advances and passes through me on his path to join the others at the table, confirming I'm not a man of substance.

"We wouldn't need you if I could still raise my arms," my great grandmother blurts out. "That damn bullet nicked my spine. Ain't been the same since."

"It's a wonder you survived," the man responded. "Unfortunately, my father did not."

"He was a good man. Shame he had to die that way. Complete waste of time. Both of us shot down and the baby taken away to Ohio. I'm just glad there's another one here. Lucky, my grandson is fertile," she finished, smiling at my uncle.

"No," I scream, "you're not going to do anything to that baby!" My words go unheard. I'm here, but I'm not, at least to the others. Somewhere in between, maybe. I can observe but nothing else.

The man lays the child on its back, just as I'd found myself. Deja vu—he speaks the same words spoken in my ceremony. I cringe as he holds the dagger high and brings it down with force to the baby's chest, stopping before penetration takes place.

Miniature energy bursts and flashes of light, dance about—engulfing the man and the child. The old woman smiles and sits up straight as the magical light show surges in her direction creating an aura around her. As she absorbs the baby's energy, her face grows younger--the years melting away. Pulling away the dagger, the man steps back seeking my great grandmother's approval.

"Damn," shrieks my great grandmother as she rises to her feet and tosses off the cane, "I feel almost young again!"

"You sure she'll lead a normal life," my uncle asks as he picks up his child and holds her close. "Normal, like any other person, no side effects?"

"The child will be fine. I've only taken twenty years from the end of her life. She'll appreciate that as old age creeps up and she suffers from arthritis and rheumatism. And, you'll never have to worry about money. I have more than enough set aside for you. Buy your family a new home. Buy your wife a car and get yourself a new one, too. And, when Julie gets old enough, buy her one!"

A feeling of being lightheaded sets in. After three times, I know I'm on my way out of this place. Blurry eyed, I catch a glimpse of my uncle and great grandmother hugging—Julie being held between them. The adults are smiling, yet, baby Julie is staring my direction and frowning.

I wake up back in front of the computer. At least I didn't hit my head this time. I regain my senses and see the finger still pointing in my direction. I close the file and light a cigarette, digesting what I had seen. Deep in thought, I take a walk in the night air—staying alert enough to sidestep the Mt. Everest miniatures of dog shit on the sidewalk left by my loving neighbors' pets.

I joke about the acid flashbacks. I know that's not the cause of what's happening. I've had two visions, both so real they scared the hell out of me—and I don't scare easy.

I want to discuss these photos with my newly found cousin. Did she suffer the same visions as I when she saw them, and if so, why didn't she warn me what to expect? Is she sharing a deep family secret, or just screwing with my head. Could there be subliminal messaging going on? Or, could she really be suffering from a ceremony originally meant for me? If so, is she seeking vengeance?

Nothing like delving into the realm of the crazed and mysterious to fuck up one's evening, is there?

Flabbergasted, I return to my computer. Back online, I'm surprised by a message from my dear, sweet cousin.

When will you finish looking at the pictures?

"Soon," I type back. "How did you know I haven't?"

I just had a feeling, that's all. I want you to see mine. It may surprise you.

Snidely, I type, "I'm hoping you're wearing clothes in it."

Of course, I do. You're not a pervert, are you? Don't answer that. Go open up my picture.

I want to ask her questions but decide to do as she ordered first. No sense in getting a new relative upset over a little thing. I hope she will still be around after I do so. Hopefully, a picture of her won't send me into another venture into the World of Hallucinations—Truth or Dare.

"Holy shit!" My words flow faster than a bad case of diarrhea. It is another picture of my great grandmother. I can tell it is a more recent photo, but she is even younger than before. Black hair instead of graying, no wrinkles on the face, and no sagging chin--she either had one hell of a makeover or I'm in trouble.

"I was wondering when you'd get off your ass and look at that one," says a voice behind me. Although not as shrill as heard previously, I know it to be that of my great grandmother. I turn my chair to face her.

"By the way, Julie sends her regards. She was happy to see I'd found you. Julie's been a big help. You know, she had four boys—three for me and one for her to replace the years she'd lost. She couldn't wait to get those back. I don't think she'd have agreed if she didn't hold such a grudge against you for getting off so easy. She doesn't think I'd have taken the years from her if

I had gotten yours to begin with. Naive, she is, but very fertile."

I try to respond but my arms and legs refuse to obey my commands to strangle the bitch. Even my mouth is frozen. Only my eyes are allowed movement. I'm stuck sitting here listening to her prattle.

"I think I look pretty good for my age. Those eighty years I stole from Julie and her family helped the cause tremendously," she snickered. "You look like you could use a few extra years. Getting old, aren't you? Already retired? My, my, it's going to be fun to see how bad you look in a few minutes when I'm done."

Prancing around the room, her happy mood is surreal. I can tell sadism is at the top of her list of things to do when bored. She's damn good at it!

"I can see you're confused. Let me explain. Magic is energy, just like electricity, or electrical impulses if you will. Wherever those travel, so can magic. All I have to do is cast a spell and catch a ride on those impulses to wherever I want to go. I save so much money on plane fair it's not funny.

Anyway, the spell cast on you was interrupted, but not ended. Spells stay active until the spellcaster ends them. So, to take twenty years of your life, all I have to do is hold up a dagger up high, like this, and bring it down close to your chest, like this!"

The loud crackling of the magical energy engulfing me fills my ears and causes every hair on my body to straighten. My strength is being drained and my muscles ache. Fingers used for typing are now crooked and gnarly, throbbing with arthritis.

The woman before me grows younger. Age disappears as her clothes hang from a now slender frame. Sagging boobs and ass reverse time and rise to once known stages of glory. If she hadn't had been my great grandmother, I would say she was one hot lady. Sadly, I've grown too old for male supplements to help me with her had I been perverted enough to do so.

"See, you really didn't escape me, no one does. No, you only postponed the inevitable. I'd love to stay and chat, but I've got things to do and places to see. Ciao!"

Without a flash or magical mist, she disappears.

I push myself up from my chair and find standing to be difficult. My knees are weak and buckle under my weight. Stumbling from chair to chair, I make my way to the adjoining hall. In front of my entry mirror, I see an older man there, one with thinning hair and brown age spots, breathing heavily from his short journey.

* * * * *

Two hours have passed since her visit. The aches and pains remain, and typing is an agonizing chore. But, I must get this message out. A warning that must be heeded.

I know I should have used my logic and not answered her first message. That knowledge does nothing for me, now. I made a mistake, a huge one, and am paying the price.

I'm weary and need sleep. Maybe, I'll wake up and be the man I was before her arrival. Maybe, this has all been a bad dream. Maybe, maybe not. I'll know when I awaken.

Maybe, I'll dream of humping my great grandmother. God, help me!

* * * * *

"Doesn't that one make you want to imagine your great grandmother wearing Spandex?"

I laughed. Sometimes, Gabriela did come out with a remark that hit home. Not often, but sometimes. "Did you ever meet your great grandmother?"

"Are you kidding? Can you imagine the family tree of a cat? Sometimes, we have a hard time knowing who our mothers are. One minute it's dark and the next minute you're grabbing hold of a nipple and doing your best to keep the other five kittens from taking it away. It's a strange life, or lives, as the case may be. But, no stranger than the story I'm getting ready to tell you. This next one isn't in chronological order, but I thought you might like to hear it. It had everybody talking in Hell. You humans may be getting ready to see what strange really is."

The Sun Rises: A Vampire's Goodbye

I wish to end my time on this planet. I'm tired, too tired to see the cycles of human ignorance and reprehensible rulers repeat themselves once more.

In my early years as a vampire, I earned a strong reputation for being ruthless and unmerciful. As the Master demanded much of me, his second in command, I rose to his expectations and created great fear of our kind in the lands I journeyed. Fear is a mighty weapon, one that controls actions and dictates results. I found it to be my friend on many occasions. Wherever I roamed, cowardly men filled with apprehension and shaking with fear--carrying hammers and sharpened, wooden stakes--followed. Except for the foolhardy, all whispered prayers they'd not find me. No answers, had they, to my battle my ability to hypnotize prey, engage shapeshifter skills, and utilize exceptional speed to escape their fumbling attacks and destroy them with my own. I was the superior being—always victorious.

Yes, there was the oaf called Van Helsing—a small and boring fellow—whose group ended the lives of many I had created. Surprisingly, the Master became one of his victims during their efforts to annihilate us who rule the darkness. But, that is a story that has been told too often and revised each time today's movie industry decides to spice up the event with newly invented special effect techniques.

The Master's death didn't put an end to his primary goal. Many times, we had sat discussing the odds of vampires dominating the world. It made little sense to allow men to rule with their feeble brains. Our intelligence—cultivated and fertilized by centuries of witnessing mankind's foolish acts—elevated us to a greater understanding of how to achieve success and allow all to profit. We had agreed, world domination by vampires would be the future.

We faced a major problem—our numbers were too few to guarantee success. We had to increase our efforts to bring more into the fold. The conflict stemmed from us refusing to lower the standard of excellence we exhibited by taking the common fools from the streets. We must require it be mandatory to bring in only those who demonstrate extreme intelligence and bravery. Only by doing so could we keep from making the mistakes that could end us, instead.

These types of individuals weren't only hard to locate but convincing them of our goals was difficult and most dangerous. Many balked at our ideas, choosing instead to do battle or force us to hypnotize prior to changing to avoid their injury. The intelligent performed satisfactorily under hypnosis—happy with a purpose to fulfill. But, too many of the brave warriors chose suicide by sunlight as their allegiance to God and country was more honorable to them than existing as a creature of the night.

After the death of the Master, I made the decision to concentrate only on the intelligent prospects. Men of logic became the avenue of dreams for our future. I used those already in the fold to seek out scholars—those who could recognize the benefit of having intelligence and the experience of centuries. Logical humans, they spent much time studying the options and consulting one another before making decisions. It was a long and tedious process. Yet, I believed it better to spend time with those who wanted to be a part of what we offered than waste time on those who didn't.

Regretfully, I must own up to my mistake. Ultimately, these were men of little action and too much thought. Although meticulous in choosing proper candidates, many were so focused they went without food for days on end during their quests to gain quality members. Among the living, this is but a minor problem to which they were accustomed. But, among vampires, it is act that has terrible results.

Blood frenzy, a malady from which we suffer—very similar to a shark feeding frenzy in which the urge to sate one's quest for food ignoring all else—was witnessed more often than ever before. When our hunger is not sated, the brain becomes obsessed with the smell of blood. Any by-passer qualifies as a food source and animal instinct takes control of all actions. The vampire cares not who his victim may be, nor how crowded the area. Thus, attacks in public take place, leaving the vampire in a precarious position open to retaliation by observers—often resulting in the vampire's demise. Humans had little mercy on a creature of the night drinking the blood of one of their neighbors.

I found this frustrating. Intelligent soldiers falling victim to blood frenzy was unacceptable. Even the children that some of our group had turned were taught how to avoid it. Cats, dogs, rats, and other animals weren't as tasty but could delay the blood frenzy until a better time presented itself. However, despite my constant warnings, these episodes continued, unheeded by those with intelligence, but no common sense.

My commands being ignored by these idiots caused others to laugh at me for coddling their disobedience. Ours is not a society of choice, but of following orders. Lack of respect for my leadership would not be tolerated. I had been too patient, expecting them to change, but with no penalty for those that refused. Outraged, I sent out correspondence for all to cease pursuits immediately and meet with me one month from the date of my writing. No exceptions!

As that night arrived, I found most were present. I ordered my most experienced members to seek out those absent and eliminate them from our ranks by tearing out their hearts. One of the newer, more intelligent members I had selected, dared to question my order by stating they might have a valid reason for not being present. I walked over to him, put my arm across his shoulders, and ripped off his head. As the others sat with mouths open, I vented my fury and tore his lifeless limbs from his torso. "This is what happens when you question my authority," I roared. "If you wish to live, you will do as I demand. Are there any questions?"

One fool dared to open his mouth. His head and limbs joined the others on the floor.

"There are no questions when I make a demand. Is that understood?"

Silence. My point had been made. I then reinforced my previous warnings against blood frenzy with a threat of similar consequences should my warnings be ignored. Testing them, I asked once more, "Are there any questions?" Their silence indicated they had listened. With no other purpose to hold them, I ended the meeting and sent them on their way.

I sat in the meeting chamber, staring at the remains of the two I had dismantled. I questioned how long the fear I had instilled would last, and how many would soon ignore me and do as before. Fear needed constant reinforcement, not easily accomplished before the age of modern communication tools. There had to be another answer, one that would be more effective in making my leadership and commands unchallenged.

An epiphany hit me and my days as a human child came to mind. I'd been adventurous—much to the chagrin of my mother—and often doing as I thought best instead of following her instructions. I'd go off on hikes well beyond distances allowed, climb trees much taller than permitted, and jump over crevices that even adults wouldn't attempt to cross. Wild and free, I ended up with a broken leg and confined to my bed for several months. During this time, I was often asked by visitors, "Why did you do it? Why did you ignore what you'd been told by your mother?"

At first, I laughed off their questions. I'd heard that being young was an excuse to expand upon set boundaries. Exploring one's limits had consequences, but excitement as well. Yes, I had ignored my mother's restrictions and orders. My leg in a cast, I was paying the price for doing so. Many reaffirmed the need to follow her directions in the future. That became the general message conveyed. They'd become part of her army in that my acceptance of her experience might assist in keeping me from spending time laid up, or worse, in the future.

I had become my mother. Warning and threatening only came from the one in charge—no others. I had chosen to set "my children" loose, expecting them to comply. The recent acquisitions had been somewhat effective in locating and recruiting men of intelligence, but many had ignored basic commands. My older members, although not as educated, followed my commands without hesitation. Neither group, on their own, was effective in producing the army we would require. An answer comprised of common sense came to me and I asked myself, "Why don't I utilize their talents separately, instead of lumping them together?"

I had fallen victim to the viewpoint of vampires being one group of soldiers under one leader. Yet, history teaches that every great commander had his generals, advisers, support personnel, and soldiers. A complete reorganization was in order if we were to succeed.

I studied the structure of the Roman Legions, French and British military, and even the hordes of Genghis Khan. Traveling Europe, I sought descriptions for all duties and responsibilities of each position and deliberated for hours over who I should select for each slot?

During my travels, I met with those chosen for major leadership roles. My instructions were made clear and their understanding found refreshing. Happy with their advancement, each promptly began to fulfill their responsibilities.

The numbers of the fold steadily increased. My generals did the locating and planning and the soldiers the stalking and collecting. Blood frenzy events vanished. All was proceeding better than expected.

Turning my attention to successful revolutions, I discovered most revolved around the inequality of the rich and poor. Greed was a constant in all cases as both rich and poor were never satisfied. There was the "more, more, more" factor they had not learned to control. Humans had never recognized that unless all is portioned equally, greed will breed hatred and contempt in those that have little, for those that have it all. That is a fact that holds true to this day.

Europe was a constant cycle of royalty and peasants. True, middle class citizens raised themselves from the mire of the streets and hopes of possible opportunity teased the minds of the lower class. Yet, European society was condemned to a life of habit, a society that refused to learn from its mistakes. A society doomed to returning circles.

Although scoffed in public, superstitions were the one thing that could bring the public together. We creatures of the night had stopped being tales told to scare children. Instead, we became threats that were hunted and murdered while we slept. As time continued, we lost two for every new vampire we gained. Although Europe had always been my home, I decided it was time to seek other breeding ground where the danger wasn't as great.

A country had formed across the ocean by those dissatisfied with the European Royalty's increasing taxation and ridiculous demands. This nation had grown at a tremendous rate and offered freedoms unavailable in Europe. My curiosity commanded me to explore this new land. So, I bid adieu to Europe's shores and headed west.

The journey across the ocean took much longer than promised. I shipped myself in a wooden crate supplied with a sufficient amount of blood in sealed jars. I've never been one to appreciate congealed blood, but I had few options if I wanted to avoid discovery. To make matters worse, the delays caused by tumultuous seas and terrible storms, as well as several days of the doldrums, required rationing myself to the minimum needed to avoid blood frenzy. I was famished when the ship finally arrived in port.

A night watchman provided a fine meal upon my bursting from the crate later that evening. I tore at his throat and feasted on the warmth of his blood—as a wolf would a young fawn—with the illumination of a full moon casting shimmering reflections of the Delaware River upon me. Hunger sated, I sat inhaling the stimulating aromas of Philadelphia. It is my first memory of this new land. One I still cherish.

I made a slave of a lamplighter, who rented a house for me under the guise of being a traveling scholar's advance servant. My habit of sleeping during the day and only going out at night created suspicion, but I laughed it off as an eccentricity of mine to those who asked. If questioned further, I begged for discretion in keeping my skin allergy to the sun's rays a secret one—knowing this would be shared with all in the area within hours. Apart from a few rambunctious school children, my slave would chase away, I was left undisturbed.

I enjoyed evenings in the city. Although not as cultured in opera and orchestral presentations as Europe, this new land offered an entertaining and fresh approach. Traveling up to New York, a world of opportunity exceeded my expectations. New York provided a constant parade of potential members for our fold, as well as an abundant food source.

As suspected, I discovered it easier to grow my army here. The United States populace scoffed at old country superstitions and called them tales of fantasy and illusions of fiction. Naive, many found the truth too late and others now live the fantasy as one of us.

The changes I have seen in this country over the last century have been phenomenal for our growth. Perhaps the greatest help has been Hollywood's portrayal of our kind. No longer are we regarded as the bloodthirsty killers that slink in the darkness, but rather individuals who simply wish to survive among the living. These types of movies and television series, several written by members of our fold, have created "fans" for our cause. These believers volunteer to serve us and provide for our needs. Their support has made both selection of new members and feeding much easier. Many have nighttime occupations such as club management, food preparation, hospital duties, and even security personnel. All have made it easy to merge into society.

Soon, our numbers will allow us to achieve our goal of world domination. For centuries, I'd planned on overseeing this world takeover. Yet, my desire to be the one to assemble and initiate change has left me. Perhaps, I am tired of the battles I've fought. Perhaps, I'm tired of mankind's repeated ignorance.

Vampires work endlessly for the benefit of the fold as all are deemed equally important. Man works only to increase his bank account, caring little to none of those he hurts along the way. He has learned nothing from history's mistakes, egotistically believing he is much wiser than those preceding him. Even today, the reduction and planned elimination of the Middle Class by the rich will lead to another revolution. I wish not to see what instrument of death replaces the guillotine of old, nor the arenas that replace the town squares for the executions forthcoming.

I have named my successor. He is ready and able to accept the task. I know he will succeed. Our numbers are too great and the stupidity of mankind too prevalent. Combining vampires and human slaves in our army, our preparation has left no weakness for any result other than the one we've planned.

So, you have your story. I have no fear of you publishing it whenever you wish. The words will only be lost in the mass of hate and propaganda your media presents at the orders of your government. Your leaders do so to keep the power of those they rule divided, a distraction while they do as they please to ensure their power and wealth stay intact. We vampires sit back, recognizing that common sense has been defeated by fear and hate, as emotions are mistaken for intelligence. That will be your final downfall. The circles will cease. Our domination will be swift.

The morning sun is struggling to make its entrance to begin a new day. See, it lightens the darkness above the mountain range. I haven't watched a sunrise in centuries. I'll cherish the sight as long as I can—before my body is consumed in flames. This is a fitting end for a creature of the night.

I thank you for being alongside. It's nice to have company. When my kind takeover, you inform them I had you along to tell the world my story the way it should be told. It will serve you well. I'm sure your death will be quick.

* * * * *

"I'm going to tell you one more story about a previous owner. This one may shock you a little. It's not one of my favorite tales to tell."

"So, what's wrong with this story? Is it as bad as some of the others you've already told?"

"No, but with the constant focus on the living dead, I'm not sure if it will bore you," Gabriela looked somewhat reluctant to tell me more until I pushed her

further. "There's not much to be told that hasn't already been the plot of a television show or low budget movie."

"Well, there hasn't been an outbreak of a virus strain that changed the whole human race into zombies, so that can't be a factor," I joked.

"Those shows are so fake," she shot back. "How anyone can believe them is beyond me. No, this is a story that took place in the '90's, before all the junk hit Hollywood. If you're interested, I'll tell it. If not, I'll tell you some more of the ones I've been told. It's up to you."

" Let's hear it. I just hope I'm not sorry when you're done."

"You're sorry anyway, especially that crap you used to write. Now, if you're ready …

Cat's Paws

Don Blevins hated driving back and forth each week. Still, the educational system in Southern Alabama was superior to that in Baton Rouge. In fact, everything was better—lifestyle, lower crime rate, less traffic, cheaper housing, even entertainment. It was as if those living in Baton Rouge believed themselves to be worthy of higher prices because of the close vicinity to New Orleans and all that city offered. In his opinion, if they didn't have college sports to brag about, Baton Rouge was simply another bump in the road.

Three months before, he had been offered a promotion to sales manager of the Baton Rouge district. The insurance company needed good people there but couldn't seem to find locals to fill the position. Oh, many were willing to take the job, but getting them motivated enough to do it was another story. Don had proven himself to be a great agent—conscientious and loved by all his customers. So, it was only natural for the company to offer him a promotion to retain him.

He had accepted the position, planning on moving his family there when the school year was over. He had rented a small efficiency apartment until that time. However, after getting to know the area and seeing firsthand the inflated cost of living, he and his wife agreed to keep their home in Alabama with him commuting the two hundred miles every week.

I'd been the pet of a college student for the first year of my life. Tired of having pot smoke blown in my face and going days without being fed, I booked, hoping to find another home that would better suit my needs. I was digging for food in a dumpster one muggy afternoon when Don tossed in a bag of garbage. He almost hit me with it! Not being bashful, I let him know I wasn't too pleased.

"Did you just talk to me?" he asked, a little surprised at the words I'd used to describe him. "How did you do that?"

"Does it really matter?" I replied, still pissed. "Why don't you get in here and I'll toss garbage at you, so you'll see how it feels?"

He apologized with sincerity, still somewhat shaken to be communicating with a feline. We talked a short while about my current lack of residency and my previous owner. Don surprised me when he asked, "Why don't you come live with me? I've plenty of room and you won't go hungry. You'll have the place to yourself most of the time, be protected from the elements, and if I move, you'd be welcome to come along."

Not having a better offer, I accepted. He had a small efficiency apartment in a place called Tiger Town, named after the university that sat up the road a mile or so. He'd leave early and get home late, always making sure I had plenty of food and water until he returned. At night, we'd play some while watching television, and sleep on a king size mattress he had lying on the floor. I did get lonely on weekends when he went to visit his family, but there was usually enough action in the complex to keep my attention at the window. Still, the time between him leaving on Friday and returning on Sunday evening dragged more and more as I found myself missing his company.

Yeah, even I can get attached.

As his primary job was training and replacing agents, he was constantly visiting different areas of the state. One day he might be in Hammond and the next New Roads. Shreveport was the furthest northern point of his responsibility, and Thibodaux or Gonzales the most southern. Obviously, he was on the road constantly.

One evening, Don came home having been in Simmesport all day. He was tired, but unusually quiet. Reading his mind, I could tell he had faced the family of a client that had passed away. No matter how hard he had tried to help them understand, their emotions ignored the facts. It was simple--no premiums paid meant no obligation of the company to pay a death benefit. The irate family turned their anger on him. Amid hostile threats of vengeance and injury, he escaped without bodily harm.

What scared me about the event was that these were bayou people, born and bred with swamp water in their veins. New Orleans may be the capital of voodoo, but most in the bayou know at least one practitioner that can cast a mean spell. I pushed him a little to tell me more about the threats made, but he refused to discuss them. I knew he was bothered, though, as he tossed and turned in his sleep all night.

A month went by without any fallout. Don gradually returned to the Simmesport area to assist his new agent. They'd been invited to eat dinner with a family and had enjoyed the meal. On the way home, the Cajun food started to play with his stomach some. By morning, even a closed bathroom door couldn't stop the smell of his intestinal battle. Unable to function, he called into work sick--doing the same the next day. By Friday, he had weakened terribly, even forgetting to feed me until reminded … twice. When he called his wife and cancelled his weekend trip home, I knew something was wrong.

Saturday night, Don rose from bed, got dressed, and left the apartment without saying a word. When he returned, there was blood on his hands and face. He showered and went back to sleep. The next morning, he remembered nothing about his departure.

We caught the evening news, Sunday, and listened to the anchorman report another murder in the city. With its high crime rate, this was nothing new for Baton Rouge. What caught my ear was how close to us the murder had taken place. I began to worry further when the story unfolded and there was mention of part of the body being stripped of flesh. That wasn't normal for Baton Rouge or anywhere else!

After a doctor's visit on Monday, Don returned home and again slept until late in the evening. Supposedly, his ailment was a combination of food poisoning and an allergy to crawfish. When he woke and left the apartment well after midnight, I suspected something else might be the culprit.

I can't say I waited patiently for his return. Sitting on the window ledge, I kept watch for several hours, hoping to see him walk up the steps in a normal state. When he finally appeared around the corner of the building, it was in a similar state to his return Saturday night. Again, a shower and bed, nothing else. His mind was blank, as if someone had erased what had taken place during his night's excursion. It was then I had no doubt, he was under some sort of spell.

Several days he attempted to go into work but returned to the apartment by noon. He had stopped eating, except for what I imagined he consumed during his nightly outings. Again, he called his wife on Friday, cancelling his trip home to Alabama. And, again Friday night, he left late and returned bloody.

We were awakened by a knocking at the door the next morning. Sluggishly, Don slipped on some trousers and opened it to find his wife and two daughters hollering, "Surprise!"

"What are you guys doing here?"

"Since you won't come to us, we came to you," his wife answered, smiling as she hugged him. "I was worried about you. I know you needed me to take care of you and help get you well. By the looks of you, I was none too soon. You look terrible!"

Don's wife, Amanda set to work immediately, washing his clothes and sheets, mopping up the kitchen and bathroom floors and vacuuming the carpet. She even cleaned my dishes, filling them with fresh food and water. His daughters, Mollie and Karen, played with their toys and watched television most of the time, helping their mother whenever possible. Don slept most of the day, only waking when Amanda tried to make him eat.

I stayed on the window ledge most of the day. The apartment seemed plenty big for just Don and me. But, adding three more people made it seem tiny. The few times I did walk around I had to tread lightly while others rushed about. I did receive some soft petting from Amanda, but the girls wouldn't stop tickling my ears, thinking it was funny to see my head jerk about. It was a relief when Amanda had them lay out their sleeping bags and pillows and go to sleep.

Lights out, I left the ledge and took my place on the bed—careful not to awaken Amanda. The day had been the most hectic one I had experienced since leaving the student and I was exhausted. Sleep came quickly.

I awoke to the sounds of ripping tendons.

Raising my head, I looked over to where the noise originated. By the recliner was Don, stripping the flesh from Karen's arms and devouring it piece by piece. The blood-soaked carpet glistened, reflecting the light from the nearby lamppost. I could see Mollie had already suffered death at his hands—her pajama top torn open and her chest cavity empty of its heart.

I couldn't believe the scene. How could a father kill and eat his children? Surely his love would be strong enough to fight any demon that controlled him. Yet, here Don was, engaging in the unthinkable.

The bedside lamp illuminated the scene and Amanda's scream pierced the night. An eerie grin appeared on Don's face as he rose to his feet, having chosen his next victim. Around the room they scrambled, Amanda staying just clear of his grasp. Scream after scream, she fought to escape his attacks. Kicks, punches, and bites were dealt out, yet, strong fingers clasped hold of Amanda's throat and ripped the skin apart. As the blood gushed out and life went with it, the apartment door burst open and shots rang out. Don died licking his fingers.

I ran from the apartment, not wanting to be there any longer. A spell had transformed my sensitive owner into a true member of the living dead, feasting only on flesh, no matter who the victim. Roaming the streets over the next week, I read about the story many times, thankful that I had not fallen victim, but saddened by those that had.

Ironically, I was taken in by an elderly lady who owned a small shop. She specialized in selling love potions and such to the locals that believed in those things. When I died, she cut off my feet and sold them as magic cat's paws. Somewhere today, if the owners are lucky, they're forgotten in somebody's home collecting dust. I hope it's no one's home in Simmesport.

* * * * *

Gabriela yawned and headed off to her den behind the couch.

"Hey, one question before you nap. What about your other lives? Are you going to tell my readers about them, or keep them waiting?"

Peering out, she displayed a slight grin, "Since when does a girl tell everything about herself in one sitting? Let's keep them guessing until Book Two comes out. Agreed?"

There was something about her words that made sense, if not for the readers, for my safety. Although she had calmed down since her arrival, I saw no reason to raise the ire of a sleeping demon. As usual, I did the only sane thing I could.

"Yes, agreed."

The End
… for now

About the Author

Richard "Rich" Rumple currently resides in Lexington, Kentucky, after having grown up in Indiana, with New York, Chicago, Mobile, Baton Rouge, and Europe all mixed in between. "Gabriela..." is his third effort, following the highly successful "Horror Across The Alley" and "They Lurk In Summer."

"People need an adrenaline rush from time to time, and creating that gives me one, too. It's similar to when I did stand-up comedy and got the audience laughing--there is no better feeling than to be able to take their minds off their daily problems and allow them an escape."

Gabriela

Made in the USA
San Bernardino, CA
03 December 2018